I0535510

Also by Leone Sperling

Mother's Day

Oasis

What about love?

Jamie

The Book of Life

At forty and divorced a woman journeys from Australia to Europe on a voyage to freedom and discovery. Her escape is from the past – from the demanding social and sexual roles which have trapped her all her life. In distancing herself she is at last free to examine her childhood, adolescence and marriage, to see with a new clarity her inner compulsions and driving sexuality.

This is the story of one woman's liberation, told with wit and an eccentricity of observation. It is her realization that in the Stygian passage through life she has paid more than her due, and the rest of the journey is free.

COINS FOR THE FERRYMAN is a startling first novel from a talented new writer.

Cilento Publishing is proud to release COINS FOR THE FERRYMAN, Leone Sperling's accomplished debut novel, previously not available since its first publication in 1981.

COINS
FOR THE
FERRYMAN

A novel by Leone Sperling

© Leone Sperling 1981, 2014

Leone Sperling asserts the moral right to be identified as the author of 'Coins for the Ferryman'.

First published 1981 by Pan Books (Australia) Pty Limited.

This edition published by Cilento Publishing, Sydney Australia.

Typeset and cover design by Green Avenue Design.

ISBN: 978-0-9925601-6-4

All rights reserved. No part of this publication may be reproduced, stored in a retrieval system, or transmitted, in any form or by any means, electronic, mechanical, photocopying, recording or otherwise, without the prior permission of the publishers.

For those who understand that the personal can be universal.

ONE

She has come to visit me. Bundling, grey efficiency – severe-faced, square-jawed, high cheek-boned, rouged, slim-waisted, small-breasted, neatly packaged in round-necked, pastel-coloured, candy-striped dress – my mother.

It is Friday, 10am. Her eyes dart guarded glances at my untidy lounge room. The deep, soft, gold and maroon tapestry-patterned bean-bag chairs flop in comfortable disarray. I can almost discern, in their disordered curves, the imprint of the four little bodies that, last night, nested curled in their velvet warmth.

She looks around. Her hands itch. She picks up a doll with a vegemite face. She cannot hide her distaste. She longs to scream at me, wants to shout out her disgust, ask me how I can possibly live in such a filthy, unhygienic mess. She says nothing. She keeps herself in control. I want her to shout at me so that I can shout back at her. I want her to attack me so that I can defend myself. But in my family no one shouts. We keep our screams locked carefully below throat level. Our howls reverberate in our bellies. We never, never let them out.

'Would you like a cup of coffee?' I ask politely, showing that I know how to play the game, not allowing the aggressive 'What are you doing here? What do you want?' questions to rise any further than my navel.

She can't help it. While I'm putting on the kettle she has to gather the dirty breakfast dishes, scrape the greasy bits of bacon and half-eaten toast off the plates.

'I'll just wash up these few dishes, dear,' she says, 'while you're making the coffee.'

I want to tell her not to wash them up, but the words don't come out. I feel an angry scream mounting inside me but I squash it down and make a grab for a leftover piece of cold toast before it disappears into the rubbish bin. I half chew it and swallow it down quickly to keep the scream from surfacing.

'I thought I would come and give you a hand,' she says.

'I don't need any help,' I reply. Have I actually said the words? I'm not sure. Maybe they are just the words that I would like to be able to say. She goes on as if I haven't said them so I assume I've kept quiet.

'I thought,' she continues, 'that as you're going away on Sunday, you might need some help to get things cleaned up before you leave.'

'I don't need any help.' This time I'm damned sure I've said the words out loud, but she still goes on as if I haven't. I take the biggest apple I can see in the fruit bowl and tear off an enormous bite with my teeth. I keep chewing while she talks to me.

'You don't have it easy,' she says, you girls today. Not like my day. I always had a maid to help me. Look at you – divorced, alone with four children, a big house to run, a full-time teaching job. It's not easy, not easy at all.

I swallow my mouthful of apple and take a deep breath. I speak very loudly and very clearly. 'I don't need any help.' She looks hurt.

'Thanks very much for offering, Mum, but I can do it myself.' A year ago I couldn't have said it. A year ago I'd have let her bulldoze her way through our belongings and create order out of our chaos.

She sits down to drink her coffee. 'Well, dear,' she says, 'I'll just have a cup of coffee with you before I go.' I have defied her, but now some inner force compels me to open the biscuit cupboard. My hands take out the new packet of chocolate biscuits. My fingers tear off the cellophane wrapping and then from hand to mouth the biscuits go – shove, crunch, swallow.

She pretends not to notice what I'm doing in the hope of hiding her horror. She thinks that if she ignores what I'm doing then I'll stop doing it. She's wrong. I would like to be able to stop eating the chocolate biscuits but I don't know how to do that. She keeps on pretending that she's not watching me. But I know she's watching me and that makes it impossible for me to stop. She would like to grab hold of me and shake me and make me stop. She would like to scream, 'How can you be such a pig!' But she sticks to the rules, confining her scream to her eyes.

I think I'm going to vomit. I wish I would. But I know I won't. I never vomit. My stomach's made of elastic.

'You really need to get away, dear, don't you,' she says, sympathetically.

'Yes, I do,' I reply, struggling for control.

'You know, dear,' she goes on, trying not to count the exact number of biscuits I've eaten, 'when you get to London you must book yourself up on organized tours. Believe me, it's the only way to travel. That's what Daddy and I have found. Someone else does all the worrying for you. And you meet such nice people. People who speak your own language. I mean otherwise, dear, you might be very lonely, mightn't you, going overseas for six weeks all by yourself.'

I stare at her, through her. She goes on talking. I retreat. I don't know what she's talking about. Going overseas 'alone'. What does she mean? Doesn't she see that, on my life's journey, I am constantly accompanied by two grandmothers, three aunts, five cousins, one brother, one sister, one father, an ex-husband and four children? Above all, doesn't she realize that I always carry her iron-grey image around with me? Doesn't she understand that I'll be taking her overseas with me? Hopefully I'll lose her – somewhere along the way.

She leaves and I am alone with myself and my thoughts, my house and my mess to puddle and muddle and sift through and order. And I do it, in my own quiet, chaotic way. By the end of the day I have achieved a semblance of order that my children would regard as tolerable. If the dining room table is still piled high with the favourite possessions of four small people, then who cares? We never eat at the dining room table anyway. To the five of us, our mess connotes warmth, love, friendliness. Why should we care if it offends the eye of the outsider? We are snug and warm and secure in our sea of dolls and cars and guns and books and sticky, soft caresses.

My eyes fill with tears. I allow the trickling warmth to tumble down my cheeks. Can I bear to leave them, to be separate from them, for six whole weeks? How will they manage without me? I'm forty years old. Time, surely, to go off on my own for a while – to have a look at the world, to have a look at myself. Of course they can manage without me.

Time, too, I realize, to pick them up from school. It is the last dreary day before the long summer holidays begin. My three sons come bounding out of the gate. How little it takes to make their eyes shine – a hailstorm, a rainbow, an ice cream, the last day of school. I try to look at them objectively and can't. Surely anyone would find them beautiful. The oldest boy – large, placid, responsible, almond-eyed. The second – little, nuggety, tough, aggressive, black cherry eyes. The third – precious, gentle, sensitive, blonde-curled, soft-lipped. They all want to talk at once. It's impossible. I shout for silence, allot turns (youngest first) and each boy's news bubbles out. They are all high on holidays.

We pick up the littlest one. She is waiting anxiously. Tiny, exotic, dark-haired, delicate girl-child. I pick her up and hug her and feel her little arms about my neck. She tolerates my show of affection because she hasn't seen me all day. We bundle into the car and they talk excitedly of holidays and fun, of beaches and picnics, of films they want to see, of Christmas Day at Grandma's house, of presents they might get. Suddenly someone mentions the fact that I will not be there. An appalling silence descends upon us all.

★ ★ ★ ★ ★

'I understand,' she says, with absolute assurance, 'that you need to be on your own for a while. When I grow up, she goes on, 'I'll want to be alone for a while too.'

It is Sunday. 10am. The day I am due to leave on the grand world tour. She is sitting up on the bench next to me, while I wash up the breakfast dishes. She is six years old.

I don't know what to say to her.

'Will it upset you,' I ask, 'to stay with Grandma and with Daddy while I'm away?'

'Not at all,' she replies. She goes on, 'It's perfectly natural for you to want to be alone. You might,' she adds, 'even write some more stories while you're away.' I want to dry my hands, hug her, kiss her, tell her I love her, tell her it's not her I want to leave, tell her she must know how much I love her, explain to her that its just that I need to be alone for a while, need to sort myself out, see where I'm going. But she's not asking me for reassurance, she's not begging for love, so I can't give it to her.

I go on washing-up and I listen to the chatter.

Why is she so secure and why am I so insecure? My mother's words on the telephone half an hour ago still echo in my ears – 'Not coming to the airport … such a hot day …you don't mind, do you dear? …such big crowds … not coming to say goodbye.' I am shocked numb. I cannot believe she will not come.

I finish in the kitchen and go into my bedroom to pack my suitcase. I know exactly what I'm taking so it's not a difficult task to carry out. While I'm packing my mind goes back to yesterday.

It is Saturday. 1pm. It's my last full day with the children and I want them to be happy. 'Take us to Luna Park!' they all beg and plead. I hate Luna Park. I always refuse to take them there. I must be feeling terribly guilty about going away without them because I find myself agreeing to take them. They are unbelievably ecstatic.

As soon as we get there, they make me go on some dreadful machine that twirls me into space. I am quite sure I'm going to die. I can't even open up my eyes. They laugh at my terror. They get more pleasure from my fear than they do from the monstrous contraption we're riding on. I realize how afraid I am to leave the face of Mother Earth. Yet my children can leave it with defiant laughter, positive that no harm will come to them.

They make me go on the Ferris wheel. I'm not too bad while it's moving, but it keeps stopping to let more people on. Every time it stops I feel an overwhelming urge to jump off and smash myself on the ground below. I cling on to the two littlest children as if their tiny hands can hold my compulsion down.

They look at my terror. They shriek delightedly to each other, 'Look at Mummy! She's so scared she has to hold on to us. Look at her! Look at her!'

'Don't move!' I yell at them. 'Don't move! You'll fall!' They are doubled up with laughter. The more they laugh the more they move. The more they move the more terrified I become.

I see all five of us – a mound of indecipherable arms and legs, blood, flesh, brains emptying onto the pavement.

Thank God! It's not going to stop any more – it's going to keep moving. We just might survive after all. I find it's alright when the wheel is coming downwards towards the ground but when I am drawn upwards, away from the earth, my entire being shrieks a silent protest. The ride ends. They have to help me off. I am totally disordered. They sit me down. Their laughter turns to concern. They fuss over me. 'Are you alright, Mum?' 'Do you feel sick?' 'Can I get you a drink?' I am so shattered I cannot even reply. This is ridiculous. I don't want to frighten them. This is their day. We are all supposed to be having fun. With enormous effort I pull myself back to them. I laugh at myself. 'What a stupid mother I am, to be so afraid of heights.'

They are reassured. They like me to see myself in the role of 'stupid mother'. It makes them feel more grown up. I send them off with a few dollars to buy themselves ice creams while I get on quietly with the process of knitting myself together again. By the time they get back I'm all in one piece.

I've been 'good' so far today. Being 'good' means eating healthy foods, like meat and eggs and fruit and vegetables. Being 'good' means eating no bread and no cakes and no sweets and no chocolate biscuits. I've found, to my great surprise, that there's a health food shop at Luna Park. You can actually buy yoghurt instead of hot-dogs and fairy-floss. I'm pleased with myself for having been 'good' today.

My daughter suddenly hands me a sticky, dripping ice cream. 'I've had enough,' she says. Its melting sweetness is inside my mouth before I realize what's happened. One mouthful is all it needs for me to lose the battle for the day. For the rest of the afternoon I join the children on an endless orgy or waffles, ice cream, hot chips, soft drinks, lollies and fairy-floss until we all stagger to the car. They are full, warmly satisfied. A great day. I am bloated with despair. If I cannot cope with a Ferris wheel, how the hell am I going to cope with a jumbo jet?

I come back to my bedroom and my packing and to the two biggest boys bursting into my room, asking me how much money I'll give them to spend at the airport.

They are so calm. They behave as if today were any ordinary day. I feed on their tranquility and realize that they are quite able to let me go. They know I'll come back. They know that our circle of loving will always be there – warm, complete, secure.

How I wish I could be like them, but my mother's words are still banging away there inside my head – 'Not coming to the airport' – and I am forced to face the extraordinary truth that not one of my children is bound to me as I am bound to her.

They help me put my things in the car and we go off for our final treat. We are going to a Chinese restaurant for lunch and afterwards to the airport. My plane is due to leave at 4pm.

They love Chinese food and I don't mind taking them because it's always possible to be 'good' at a Chinese restaurant. I'm happy to stick to meat and vegetable dishes. Not like McDonald's. That's a nightmare. At McDonald's I am constantly faced with the temptation of Big Macs and French fries and ice cream sundaes with hot caramel sauce. At a Chinese restaurant I feel reasonably safe.

I'm very on edge. Anxiety. Terror. Anticipation. I remind myself, between the vegetable soup and the beef chop suey, that I've never been on my own for any sustained period of time. I have gone from belonging to belonging; from school to university to marriage; from parental home to marital home;

from being a child to being a wife to being a mother. There has never been a time when I have been responsible only to myself, belonged only to myself.

I feel that I ought to reprimand my third son, who is eight years old, for shoveling beef and oyster sauce into his mouth with a spoon and a hand instead of with a spoon and a fork. I stop myself. He is having such a marvelous time, gravy all over his hands and face. The frequent reprimands of my children's father momentarily disturb me, almost prompt me to tell my son to use his fork. 'Why can't you teach them some table manners! They can't even use a knife and fork properly.' He's right. They do embarrass him when he takes them out. But if I do reprimand my son it will be with his father's voice, not my own. He's not embarrassing me. I don't give a damn. I just enjoy watching his total immersion in messy pleasure. I win over the father's voice. I say nothing to my son. No! Damn it! I haven't won at all because suddenly I'm asking my daughter if she really wants all the rice she's ordered and she gives me some and before I know it I'm shoving rice into my mouth. Now I know for certain that when I buy them an ice-block after the Chinese meal, I'll have to buy one for myself as well. They'll be satisfied with water ice-blocks. I'm going to need an ice cream, probably with chocolate coating. I sink into despair. I am nothing but my mouth. I fuse with the food. I am the food. I cannot distinguish the boundaries of my self. I cease to exist. The avalanching, rumbling monster in my belly asserts himself again.

I try to picture him. He is a lion, roaring there in the dark hollow of my insides, demanding his right to gobble people up. I don't want him to gobble people up and, above all, I don't want anyone to know that he's inside me so I keep throwing him chunks of food to keep him quiet. I know I have to come to terms with him. If he and I are both going to inhabit this body for the rest of its life then we're going to have to understand each other. It seems to me that I'm always considerate about his needs but he doesn't make much effort to understand mine. At times I've thought of trying to exorcise him. But if I got him out of myself what would be left? How would I fill the gaping hole he left behind? Would there be anything left? Or am I synonymous with my lion; are he and I one entity and if I let him die would I die too? I don't know. So I keep on feeding him — just in case.

Am I mad? I don't really know but I don't think so. It all makes sense to me. I am born under the star of Leo and I carry my sign within me. A few times I've tried to tell people about it but when I do so I sense that they think what I'm saying is peculiar so I've learned to keep quiet about it, most of the time.

I don't just buy them ice-blocks. I become generous. I let them buy peppermint creams and thin, round, dark-chocolate discs from the expensive sweet shop that is just over the road from the Chinese restaurant. They can't believe their luck but my generosity is deceptive. I'm being cunning. I know that this shop sells mouth-watering Turkish Delight. My stomach is full but there is no connection between hunger and my need to eat. I have to have the sweet. I buy a whole pound. It's terribly rich. Any normal person would be satisfied with one or two pieces. I eat the lot. In five minutes it's all gone.

I want to vomit. I long to vomit. The rich, sticky sweetness nauseates me. I feel five months pregnant, my stomach distended and sore. I berate myself. 'You disgusting gluttonous pig,' I say to myself. I become the Turkish Delight, quivering, jelly-fat. I hate myself. I long for the day to be over. Tomorrow will be a new day, a new start, a new chance.

I always long for the magic of Mondays, a new beginning of a new week and if the first of the month happens to fall on a Monday then it seems to me that I have a double chance to start anew, to be 'good'. Maybe, just maybe, I will have the strength to get through a whole week, even a whole month, without stuffing myself with food. It never happens, of course. I'm so anxious about it being Monday that I'm usually shoveling food into myself by mid-morning.

I went to a hypnotist once. He stopped me from smoking and I thought he might be able to stop me from eating. It didn't work though. Sometimes, for no apparent reason, it goes away for a while and I actually stay on a diet for months and months. I get really slim and as soon as that happens I start eating again and put on all the weight I've lost. I once told myself that if it hadn't gone away by the time I was forty I'd kill myself. I'm forty now and it hasn't gone away. I can't very well kill myself though, can I? I've got four children relying on me.

And it happened again last night. It hasn't happened for years. I had a dream. People kept coming into my room, lots of people – my brother, my sister, Mum and Dad, men I've known. They held up a big white sheet next to my bed or maybe it was a flag – yes, that's right – an American flag or a Union Jack. I thought they might wrap me up in it. Perhaps it was my shroud. But they didn't. They just held it up so that I couldn't see behind it. I heard noises, though. I knew they were all screwing behind that flag and I was all alone; no one was making love to me and I felt so lonely that I started to cry and suddenly I couldn't breathe – I was choking, choking, choking and I woke up and I was suffocating, my face squashed in the pillow and I had to use every bit of strength I've got to force myself up on to my arms, to get my face out of the pillow that was smothering me, suffocating me, killing me. I was wide awake then, wet, shaking. I'll die that way. One day I'll dream my suffocating dream and it will really happen. I know that's the way I'll go back.

I've dreamed similar dreams ever since I can remember. At one time it frightened me so much that I wouldn't go to sleep. I was eighteen years old. I was sure I was going to die if I let myself go to sleep. She had to sit on my bed and keep me calm until I fell asleep. Like a mother should - for her baby.

She thinks I've forgotten but I haven't. I remember being born. No one believes me when I say that so it's another thing I've learned to keep quiet about. But I do remember. I remember before I was born too. I remember swimming soft in the sunlight of the womb, rocked gentle, lulled, swaying in her belly. I remember that I preferred to breathe through our chord, our harmony of food and air, complete and total flow. I never wanted to be born at all. She and I – so separate, so remote, so far from understanding each other; she and I were one once, tuned in to each other's needs. I moved when she moved, stopped when she stopped, started with fright at her fears, cried when she cried, laughed when she laughed. Fused together.

No wonder I resisted her efforts to expel me. I could not understand why I shouldn't stay in there forever. She'd been quite happy about our union for nine months, why did she now jerk and move the walls of my fortress, make them hard and rigid, drain away my soft fluid bed? Dry and harsh she became, forcing me movement by movement down her hostile canal, muscles contracting upon me, pushing, pushing, pushing me out into the stabbing air, the bright-lit sterility. And in her haste to rid herself of me she didn't even notice that she'd let the cord wind itself around my neck so that the moment of my birth was fired with harsh, rasping, choking strangulation. Life and death mingled at my cold awakening on that bleak August day.

When I was a child I often dreamed of being chased and strangled by a long pink snake lady. It was not so much the chase that frightened me, not even the strangulation. What frightened me was the end of the dream, the moment when I realized that the face of the snake lady was exactly the same as the face of my mother.

★   ★   ★   ★   ★

I am at the airport. Sunday 3pm. I feel so separate from myself that for a moment I can't understand what on earth I'm doing here. They want money for lollies, drinks, to play the games on the machines. I keep doling it out. I don't care what it costs, as long as they are happy, as long as they don't cry. Please, God, if you exist don't let them cry.

I go to the check-in counter. It's a sweltering day. My clothes are wet. I have to carry a heavy sheepskin coat. Suddenly I remember a dream I had a few nights ago. In my dream I was standing, just as I am now, waiting to check in before boarding the plane. In my dream it was terribly hot, just as it is today. In my dream they called out our flight number and then read out the London weather report – 'Sleet, snow, temperatures below zero, freezing, rain.' I looked down at my clothes and saw that I was wearing a thin cotton dress and realized, at the same moment, that I had left my sheepskin coat at home. 'I've forgotten my coat. I've got to go home and get my coat!' Although I shouted and screamed I was locked in the crowd and they carried me, coatless, onto the plane. I felt the terror of knowing that when I reached London I would inevitably freeze to death.

The shock of the dream shivers through me and despite the heatwave conditions I clutch my sheepskin coat fiercely to me.

I am at the head of the check-in queue. My hand wets the plastic folder that holds my ticket, passport, traveller's cheques.

'Ticket please,' she says. I give her my ticket. I am very neurotic about my passport. I hope she won't ask for it. The reason I'm so neurotic about my passport is that I went through such trauma to acquire it. The red tape involved in digging up certified copies of marriage and divorce papers was bad enough. So was the implied insult from the Officer in the Immigration Department who felt that no adult lady could possibly be only 143 centimetres in height. But, worst of all, was my trip to the Registrar General's Department where my request for a copy of my birth certificate was met with the extraordinary reply that my birth had never been registered.

'It has to be there,' I told them. They checked again. There is a record of my older brother's birth; there is a record of my younger sister's birth. I feel negated. Wiped out. Why did they forget to register my birth? I ask them why. They say to each other:

'I thought you did it, Mummy dear.'

'No, dear, it was always your job to register the births.'

'Where do you want to sit,' she asks, 'aisle or window seat?' I am about to say I don't care when my friend interrupts. He has come to the airport to say goodbye to me and to take my children back to their father's house. He has had a premonition that my plane will crash.

'She'll sit right at the back of the plane,' he interjects, 'in the last row.' He doesn't want me to go. He thinks he loves me.

He thinks I'll screw ten different men every day. He thinks I'll forget him. He might be right. So he's invented the idea that my plane will crash. The certain knowledge of my death has come to him in a dream. He's had other dreams like this before. They always come true. Normally such foreboding would terrify me, but this time it doesn't. I tell him again that the plane won't crash and that I refuse to die. I'm not sure that I believe what I'm saying but by now I feel swept along too far to turn back. I've got a real sense of inevitability right now. I just know that I am going to get on that plane and go.

My third little boy flings himself into my arms and has started to give me the 10,174 kisses that he has calculated he will require to see him through the next six weeks. He is the only one I am worried about. He seems to need me so much. I know the others are self-assured enough to cope. We peck at each other, little mouth kisses, lip to lip, endlessly building his fortress of love. I suddenly wonder how he'll manage to shit while I'm away. He has some anxiety about shitting. He never does it at school or at anyone else's place. He always waits for me. 'Start me off,' he says. That means I have to stand at the toilet door while he starts. After the first 'plop' he's safe and tells me I can go away. Can he go for six weeks without a shit? I don't suppose he can. It's better than it used to be. I used to have to sit on the floor outside the toilet and talk to him the whole time.

Sometimes he develops a compulsive sniff, or his eyes twitch, or he looks at the palms of his hands and then at the soles of his feet. The symptoms are always on the move. He never sticks to any of them for too long. And he can't drink any soft drink if anyone else has drunk out of the bottle and he can't eat his dinner if anyone else breathes on it. And, above all, he can't bear to look at straight arms. No one in the family is allowed to hold their arms out straight. I don't know why. But we all understand about his little peculiarities and he has managed to carve out for himself an area of tolerance that is given to no one else in the family. He gets migraines, too, but we all ignore them. He just lies upside down on the big bean-bag chair and falls asleep and he's all better in an hour or two. I've asked the other kids to look after him but will the adults who mind him understand? He lives on some other level of reality. He just visits us occasionally but whenever he comes to call he needs so much reassurance and love before he flits off again to his own, more interesting, realm of existence.

We're up to kiss number 764 when I suddenly hug him to me. Precious, curly-haired, ageless child. 'You'll be alright, won't you?' I ask fiercely.

'Seven-hundred-and-sixty-five, seven-hundred-and-sixty-six,' he goes on, unable to be distracted from his compulsive counting.

Everything to him is a matter of numbers. As soon as he meets someone he wants to know how old they are. He's not being rude. He just needs a new jumping off point for his endless calculations. The patter goes something like this: 'If you're twenty-four years old then you're three times as old as I am and you're fifty-two years younger than Grandpa and sixteen years younger than Mummy. You might think I'll never be half your age but when you're thirty-two, I'll be sixteen and then I'll be half as old as you are.' It doesn't stop there. It goes on and on. At first you feel some need to check his calculations. Then you realize you're not supposed to do that. There's no doubt that he's right. You just have to keep nodding your head and mumbling, 'Yes'. He can't read very well and when he writes he holds his pencil in such a peculiar way that his letters emerge on the page as a spidery code of hieroglyphics. He thinks he isn't clever. I suspect he's a genius. We are up to kiss number 801. I go on and on because that's what he needs and I resist the desire to crush my warmth and my love into his little body.

'That'll do,' he says. 'I don't need as many as I thought I did.' I am relieved. I have visions of myself not being able to board the plane because we have not reached the magical number that will set him free.

My friend stands beside me, bleak. As my flight number is called he hugs me to him and I feel his tears on my cheek. Then I start to cry and I am bewildered. The children do not cry and they do not understand why we do. I have been so worried that they would be the ones to break down and now the sight of this adult crying absolutely undoes me. I break away from him and give my children a final hug. The two smallest ones are silent. I sense their state of shock. 'Have a good time,' the two big ones say, almost in unison, embarrassed by my tears.

I look at her, the littlest. In her tense eyes I see the wish to rush after me. She grabs her biggest brother's hand. He helps her hold herself back. She would like to spring from the crowd of people and dive into the plane with me. My last sight is of her tiny face, lips firmly pressed, holding back. I can't risk turning around. I dare not look at them again.

TWO

I am not ready for my first encounter with the Customs men, who demand my passport, take my hand luggage, frisk me, put metal detectors over me. I am in a dream. I board my plane and take my seat. 'I've left my children behind,' I mumble to the lady sitting next to me, in some attempt to explain my weeping.

Dapper young men walk up and down the aisles, showing people to their seats, stowing hand luggage away, offering orange juice and wet towels. I allow myself to be distracted. I am not, at this moment, afraid. I have decided that I will not, at any time, look out of the window. I will simply pretend that I am taking a very long bus ride.

The plane gathers speed as it rushes along the runway and although I've indulged in numerous fantasies of the plane bursting into flames at this point of time, I find that the actuality of the take-off doesn't scare me at all. I swing easily from the certainty of crashing to death to the certainty that I will survive. When they bring the first meal around I eat only the meat and vegetables and drink a cup of coffee. I resist the potatoes, sweets and bread rolls.

It takes a while to settle down, to get over the emotional departure, to come to terms with the fact that I'm really on my way to London. I'm quite enjoying myself and find that I'm actually brave enough to look out of the window. I am amazed at myself. I feel a kind of exultation, as if I've overcome some enormous barrier. I have let myself leave the earth. I am out on a limb, off by myself for the first time.

Not quite the first time, I recall, and my mind goes back to that earlier flight of independence and I struggle again to understand that premature take-off.

She's told me, often enough, of that early suicidal flight in the area of darkness, in the time before words. She thinks I don't remember it but I do. 'You were only four months old,' she says. 'How could you remember it?' But memory is not a matter of actual recall but a matter of feeling and there is always the world of the dream. There is the dream of the Viking mask, black-horned, red shark teeth dripping blood. And there is the dream of the little girl who is sitting with her feet dangling into the water and the sharks are swimming round and round her and if she doesn't draw up her legs they'll eat her up.

And she is there, holding me – the stone mother, steel-nippled – no wet-warm nuzzling, no gentleness, no play. She holds me, forcing the nipple, firm, milk-hot into my mouth. I arch my back. I turn my head away. She is relentless. She follows my mouth and pushes her ready breast between my clamped lips. My monstrous rage mountains, erupts, screams. I shriek. The more I turn away the more she pursues me. The room is dim. The blinds are pulled down. There is only her and me and the cool darkness of the closed room. I feel her body tense with mine. She is determined to win. She will make me feed. I turn away. She is afraid that if I do not feed from her then I will die. I will not feed from her. Whatever she does, whatever trick she tries, I will not feed from her.

We are still one, she and I. It is still the time of the fusion. I do not know that I am separate from her. Only she knows that. Her anxiety is overwhelming. She must subdue me. I turn away.

Her face is still my world. She is the source of the sun. Her skin is my skin. She is everything to me. But something in our oneness is out of tune and the part of us that is me senses our disharmony and the mouth in me that should suck the milk from her cannot, cannot, cannot … I turn away.

I am dying. She cannot understand why I am dying. She cannot believe that I will allow my life to slip away. My belly aches in its emptiness but I cannot, cannot feed. It terrifies her to see me slide away. If I should die, she would be responsible. It is her milk that must keep me alive. She refuses to let me die. She pumps her milk from her breasts and puts it into a bottle. She shoves the bottles into my mouth but I sense her milk, sniff it, smell it. I turn away. Neither she nor I will give in. We repeat the same actions, fight the same battle, day after day after day.

She is terrified. She is now quite sure that I will die. She decides to retire from our struggle and puts me into a hospital and she leaves me there. Now others take over the forcing, prizing my lips open, pushing teats between my tightly resisting jaws, bruising my baby gums. And I give in. Finally, I give in. I become a good girl. I eat.

The dream of the hospital constantly recurs in countless, aching images of darkness and hunger and death. Was she the sharks who swam about me so that I had to withdraw myself or be eaten alive? Was I the Viking Death Mask, my red biting jaws devouring the mother's breast? Was it her fault or was it mine? Did she want to destroy me or did I want to destroy her? Or did we each sense in the other a deep and terrifying aggressive force?

There are no words to express the time before words; there is only the feeling of being swept again into the infinite blackness. They have come around again with tea and cakes and I eat the cakes in the false hope that I can fill the empty spaces.

I have been on the plane now for eight hours and I'm really very tired but they never let you sleep. If you're dozing they even wake you up to see if you want anything. I would like to sleep but soon we will land at Singapore airport and I'm very excited about the fact that we've almost reached a stopover point. The plane feels cramped and restricting and I long to stretch my legs.

We touch down. Some people look as if they're going to stay on the plane. I can't understand them. Their attitude seems to me to be totally unadventurous. I silently curse my neurotic friend. It's going to take me twenty minutes to make my way to the exit up front. Why didn't I protest against his absurd need to put me right back here? Why didn't I assert myself? Because I never do, I suppose.

While I am making my slow way to the front of the plane, I am momentarily threatened by claustrophobic fear. What if the plane should blow up at this moment? What if a fire broke out? What if some unspeakable horror occurred like a man going berserk with a hatchet and chopping people up? How would I escape, sandwiched as I am? I call this the German-Jew fantasy because I always extend it to the ultimate in punishment – what if I were squashed, limb to limb, with my fellow Jews in a German gas chamber?

I suppose all Jews indulge in this fantasy from time to time. What if my grandfather had not left Poland in 1901? What if I'd been born in Europe in 1937, instead of in Australia? What would my fate have been then? I tell myself that I would have been one of the few survivors but part of me longs to be the suffering Jew. Is it a genetic heritage that we Jews love to suffer? Would I have stood there, by the side of my bearded Jewish Rabbi, prepared to die for my faith? Would I have become the sacrificial lamb? How I envy them, those Jewish ancestors of mine – centuries and centuries of persecution. They could, in the name of their beliefs, destroy themselves. But what justification do I have for self-destruction? There are no Germans hunting me. They've finished with the Jews – they're on to the blacks. These days, we Jews have to carry out our own persecution. I am saved from annihilation by my arrival at the exit door.

A pretty Singapore hostess directs us down the steps and we pile into an airport bus. We stream out of the bus and into the air terminal. There is barely time to mill once around the air terminal before we are called back. We push our way up the steps and onto the plane and I make my slow way back to my seat. With a sense of relief I sit down again. I begin to understand why the more seasoned travellers have stayed on the plane. I feel somewhat disillusioned by my first taste of the exotic East.

As we take off, I chat, in a superficial and friendly fashion, to the lady next to me. Does she, I wonder, indulge as I do in such weird fantasies? She is Canadian but she lives in Australia. She is going to meet her husband in Amsterdam and then go with him to visit her family in Canada. She will spend Christmas with them. How nice.

I realize that she is very far removed from my fantasied fellow traveller. I was supposed to sit next to a charming, sensitive, intelligent, creative, good-looking, sexy, unattached, forty-five-year-old male. He and I were supposed to look at each other and know immediately that the whole of our lives had been leading to just this moment of recognition. We were supposed to find each other's minds scintillating, exciting and stimulating. After some hours of getting to know each other, during which time conversation never lagged, we were supposed to touch hands, as if by accident. At the moment of our touching a sense of physical thrill would pulsate through each of our separate bodies and we would recognize, in an instant, that, not only were we spiritual and intellectual mates, but that our bodies belonged to each other. We would then spend the rest of the trip to London talking, whispering, touching, our physical excitement mounting by the hour until we arrived in London, dashed by taxi to the nearest hotel, tumbled into bed, reached a perfect, harmonious, unified orgasm within three minutes and lived happily ever after.

I console myself with the thought that I might meet my Knight in Shining Armour in London instead of on the plane – a small miscalculation on my part.

If only they would let you sleep! It's 1am Sydney time and they're actually going to show us a movie. John Denver and George Burns prance across the tiny screen. I can't bear to watch them. Then I realize they've turned out the lights in the cabin and that no one is going to disturb me for the next hour and a half so I let my eyes close.

I am woken by a sudden movement of the plane. We are shaking! I see the 'Fasten your seat belt' sign. I dare to take a look out of the window. A panorama of lightning fills the sky and we shake and tremble our way through an electrical storm. I know now that this is the end. I really am going to die. I project myself into the movie screen. I become John Denver and George Burns.

The storm subsides. As it does I remember that I have always believed I would live to be very old. Wishful thinking, I suppose. At my abysmally slow rate of development it will take me until I'm fifty to reach any kind of state that I would regard as mature or grown up. I want to spend at least thirty years enjoying what I will have taken fifty years in finding. Otherwise it would be grossly unfair. I let my panic subside and take a firm hold on the concept of my own longevity.

Now they encourage us to sleep. Again I drift and doze. I am eight years old and I'm playing the game. It's years since

I've thought about the game. It's a strange game and I direct it. There is a large rectangular area in the school playground. It is enclosed by a fence of benches. Inside this area there are bushes and trees. I have made this area into a body and I direct the other little girls in our play. We are little people manipulating the bodily functions of our large imaginary figure. We pull imaginary cords that make it talk, we feed it gum leaves and we help it to digest its food and then we make it piss and shit. And that's the part we love most. We make it shit, over and over again.

Why do I think of the game now? I suppose I am just trying to remind myself that once there was time when I was in control, when I determined action, both my own and the actions of others. I was not always the thing I am now, not always just the mere reflection of other people's directions.

I try to wake up but I can't. I keep floating away. I am ten years old. It is my birthday and I am crying. I am crying, I tell my mother, because I've reached double numbers and I don't want to grow up. I want to stay a child, but my breasts are already budding and pubic hairs spring unwanted on my baby mound. My fat great-uncle has just left my birthday party. He has forgotten his umbrella and I run after him. They all think I'm being good because I'm rushing after him to give him his umbrella back. But they're wrong. I have a compulsive urge to poke his umbrella into his ballooning stomach. That's why I'm rushing. In my haste I slip and fall and cut my chin. They can't stop the bleeding. I don't cry because I deserve the pain. I have been punished for my wish to poke fat great-uncle in the stomach. My parents take me to the doctor. My mother holds my shoulders and my father holds my feet while the doctor sews two stitches into the gash in my chin. I have the distinct memory of my unheld stomach jumping up in the air. I know for certain that I did not cry.

They wake us up for breakfast. Even I am sick of food. We touch down at Kuala Lumpur. The plane stops for refuelling but they do not allow us to get off. It is twelve hours now since we left Australia and I feel as if I've been on the plane for days. Bahrain, Amsterdam, London – still a long way to go. My back aches, my hips ache. I'm glad I'm so small. How uncomfortable tall people must be. At least I can stretch out my legs. We take off again to the now anticipated accompaniment of orange juice and wet towels. I try to read but can't focus on the print. I doze again.

I am still ten years old. I am in my brother's room. He is twelve years old. The boy next door is with him and they are teasing me. I long to be one of them. I would give everything to be a boy. I wear my brother's old, discarded shorts and spend my pocket money on guns. I disdain dolls and the feminine pursuits of my younger sister. I beg to join football games in the street. I climb trees. I am, in my own mind, a boy. My mother calls me a Tom-boy. I don't want to be a Tom-boy. I want to be a real boy. They keep on teasing me and then suddenly they grab hold of me and tip me upside down. They pull down my pyjama pants and then fall about the floor, rolling with laughter. I pull up my pants and blunder out of the room. I am filled with the unfairness of it all. They, who are twelve years old, have not yet reached puberty while I, by some strange European-Jewish fate, I, at ten years of age, have been shown up, caught, revealed as a potential woman. I burn with shame, aggression, despair. They have caught me out. They laugh at my no-penis. I want to die. I wish I had farted in their faces.

My breasts keep growing and my mother tries to tell me what will happen to me, what becoming a woman means. I refuse to listen. She says something about bleeding. I stop up my ears. I will not be a girl. I walk round with my arms folded so that no one will see my breasts. No one else in the class has breasts.

My sister and I are going to a party. We are dressed in little girl white muslin dresses with big sashes. Our long hair is in sausage curls tied in two bunches with thick satin ribbons. I go to the toilet and I see it – a stain of fresh red blood on my pants. I put my pants in the dirty linen basket and put on another pair. I am shaking. We go to the party and I repress what has happened to me but when I get home I know from the wetness between my legs that I'll have to go and have another look. It's real. It hasn't gone away. I put my pants in the laundry basket and put on another pair. Over the next few hours I repeat these actions until I realize that I'm going to run out of pairs of pants. So I go and tell my mother that I'm bleeding and then I wish I'd told her before because she's very helpful and she gives me a sanitary belt and pad to wear and she explains how often I should change it and how to wrap it up in toilet paper and throw it away. She makes me feel I've joined her. She has to go through this every month. She tells me I can't go swimming when I've got it. I'm still a bit confused but, on the whole, I feel we share a secret. I hate her, though, when the next day my Polish grandmother hugs me and says, 'You're a woman now.' She's actually told my grandmother. To my ten-year-old mind she has committed the ultimate act of betrayal.

The next day is Saturday. It is a warm, sunny day and normally we would go to the beach. What am I going to say? If I say, 'I can't go swimming today,' my brother and sister will ask,

'Why not?' I decide that I can only cope with the situation by pretending to be sick.

But I am saved by a very curious and unusual happening. On that very day my parents take us to buy a dog. We've never had a dog and they've decided that every boy (meaning my brother) needs a dog. He is an ugly Bull Terrier and I love him with deep passion. He ends up being my dog rather than my brother's. I get up early every morning to fill in the holes he digs in the garden every night. I sit for hours with him in the sun. My favourite activity is to put his aggressive maleness to sleep and then to sit beside him, stroking him in quiet contentment. I can fill in the holes in the garden but I can't repair the damage he constantly wreaks on the daily wash. He systematically tears our pyjamas and sheets to shreds. One afternoon, when we are all out, my parents have him taken away.

I loved him. He helped me over a difficult time and I've never forgotten how he saved me from the embarrassment of my first period. Strange to think of him now, after all these years.

I move in my seat. I am suddenly aware that memory and reality are one. My period has started. I get up to go to the toilet. It must be early but I don't really know. I never know when my period is due.

The trip is interminably long. They bring another meal. I start to realize why. People would get anxious and bored if they were not constantly fed. I try to read again. This time I make a real effort and find that I can concentrate. I don't want to drift back again. Enough of the past. I am here and it is now. I'm not a child of ten, I'm a woman of forty, off to see the world.

My neurotic friend, who has successfully stowed me away in the back row of the plane, right next to the toilets, has also forbidden me to leave the plane at Bahrain. If the plane has not crashed by the time I reach Bahrain then it is almost certain that the Arabs at the airport will gobble up a little Jewish lady like me. I decide to defy him and leave the plane. Besides, the coming of my period has brought me a feeling of elation. It is often so for me − the almost suicidal pre-period depression gives way to a high swing to ecstasy. People say it's physical but I don't believe that's so. I think that every month I act out the same thing. I am still ten years old and I still don't want to be a woman and my refusal to accept that I am a woman fills me with depression and despair. Then my period starts and with joy and relief I accept my female self.

I walk around the airport. There is really time to get a bit of exercise. The Arabs look at me and I look at the Arabs. These Arabs look more primitive than the Arab lover I once had. He was clever and intellectual and very white. These Arabs are dark and swarthy. Are they looking at me because they can tell I'm Jewish? I don't think so. I think they're looking at me because I'm wearing an Indian shirt with no bra. Suddenly I like the fact that my breasts are showing and that primitive men are looking at me. Makes a nice change from the logical, intellectual men I always get involved with. I swing up and down the airport with an enormous sense of vitality. I feel strong and wild and free. It is with great reluctance that I re-enter the plane.

THREE

Bahrain to Amsterdam. It's no good. I've tricked myself. I only thought I felt free. I can tell that I'm not free from the moment they start walking down the aisles with the trolleys. I eat all that the smiling steward puts in front of me. My only consolation is that the other people on the plane are doing exactly the same thing and they can't possibly be hungry either.

I am agitated. My dog keeps intruding, shoving his pink-eyed, ugly face into my thoughts. Why couldn't she have given him a bit longer? Why did she have to take him away from me? I see myself again sitting with him in the sun. Is it his anger that I stroke away or is it my own? If she punishes him for his aggression, what will she do to me? Will I be punished too? Will she bundle me up, one afternoon, while no one's looking, and send me off to meet some unknown fate? I think she could do it, so I keep quiet.

I remain the good girl, but my insides are rumbling with anger. This monthly dripping of blood between my legs is like an amputation. I now have no chance of growing up to be a man. The pads I have to wear to catch the blood irritate me. I can't stop touching them. I rub my fingers on my cunt and smell the stale blood. I can't leave myself alone. The blood on the pad dries hard, reddish brown. It fascinates me. I examine it minutely, touch it, sniff it, taste it, assess how much I've bled. I have to wrap up the smelly used pads and put them in the bin next to the toilet. I don't want to throw them away. The blood clogs my pubic hairs into little stiff nodules. I unstick the hairs, rubbing the dried blood between my fingers. I want to stink.

He is thirteen years old and he is now a man. He has just performed his Barmitzvah in a crowded synagogue. There are tears in my mother's eyes. His voice is unbroken, pure and high.

He sings his portion of the Jewish law with confident authority. My grandmothers both weep, one thick and foreign, the other Irish and shaky-voiced. I look down at my father shuffling in his seat, puffed pride, nervous tic in one eye, sniffing loudly. The men are downstairs and the women are upstairs. We Jewish women do not even say 'I do' at our weddings. Our husbands crush a glass beneath their feet to symbolize our fate. The God of Abraham, Isaac and Jacob, my father's father's father. Harsh and male is the Israelite God.

No manhood for me. No 'Today-I-am-a-Barmitzvah-boy' speech, no showering of praise, no mountain of presents. And no meccano set. He's waited four years for his giant meccano set, but I'll never get a meccano set, no matter how long I wait. My hips are too wide to fit into his shorts. The guns and knives and water pistols that I used to love no longer satisfy me. I don't like my dolls. There's nothing I want to play with except his meccano set and he won't let me play with that. He sends me fetching and carrying and I obey him because he's my big brother. I get sick of being his slave so I grab my little sister and we go out onto the small front verandah. We pull down our pants and, bums touching, we piss all over the potplants. She catches us and we are punished. It is the only time my mother ever smacked me. She does not believe in aggression, not even in herself.

My only consolation is that I am clever. I am so clever that I got to a special school for clever children. My sister goes there as well. That fact that I go to such a school and that my brother did not go there does not lead me to any logical conclusions concerning our respective abilities. He is, in my eyes, always cleverer than I will ever be.

We are Jews and the slaughter of our people is never forgotten in the driving force that motivates our father in his endless encouragement of our intelligence and our academic achievements. My sister and I are girls and will never have my brother's value but we are still pushed on by our father's desperate need to live his intellectual ambitions through his children. My father: conceived and born in Poland in 1900. In 1901, his family forced to flee an already threatening storm. They escape to America, then to Canada. No country; no belonging. My grandfather is an army officer with no trade, no skills, forced to leave his home because he had been helping his fellow Jews to leave Poland. Now he is lost in the ghettoes of New York. He takes a job in a clothing factory, pretending that he is a cutter and they throw him out after one day. But he learns something. He takes another job. This time he lasts three days. He learns a little more. Each job lasts a little longer; each time he increases his skills. In 1910, they migrate to Australia, the land of opportunity. Ironically, it is a Lebanese Arab who sets my grandfather up in business. They struggle with poverty. My father must leave school when he's fourteen years old, so must his sister and his brother. His mother must sit at her sewing machine at home. They win the battle for survival but my father never forgets. He never forgets that he was always top of his class in mathematics. He never stops reading, never stops educating himself. He applies his intelligence to his business and proves to be an excellent business man. The only thing that stops him from becoming extremely wealthy is that he possesses the rare quality of total honesty. He is known to other clothes manufacturers as 'the whitest man in the trade'.

We see very little of him because he is always working either for us or for the Jewish community. Only Sundays. He takes us out every Sunday afternoon, to Watsons Bay or the Botanical Gardens or the Zoo. He always buys us an ice cream and a packet of Smith's chips. My mother never comes. Sunday is her day off.

He is determined that we will all go to university and we are not allowed to entertain the possibility of going into his business. He makes this quite clear, from the time we are very small. I do my best to fulfil his dream. He is the only man I have ever respected.

I'm his little girl, his special favourite. I sense that my mother and my sister both resent the attention he showers upon me. But they have each other. They are one. They understand each other and I feel shut out of their closeness. My brother has no worries, because he is the oldest and he is the son.

My mother encourages us too. We sit every night with her, doing sums and spelling. She is a university graduate, a pharmacist. She wanted to be a doctor. She even won an exhibition to study medicine, a rare achievement in her day, but her mother wouldn't let her take it, on the basis that no Jewish man would want to marry a woman who was a doctor.

She does not encourage anything creative. To her, achievement lies in science and mathematics and good spelling. Success is getting high marks. Life is real and earnest, a very serious matter. I seldom see her laugh. She does not play with us. She does not cuddle us. We have to be good at things. She wants us to be accomplished. We have swimming lessons and horse-riding lessons and tennis lessons and piano lessons. I don't like any of these because we only do them so that we will be good at them. We wouldn't do anything for fun. To my mother, life means getting a just reward for hard work but she values the hard work for its own sake, even without a reward. It seems that the concept of happiness does not enter this reckoning. She keeps us hard at work and hard at play.

For me, school is the great escape. I love being there. I like the intellectual challenge, the aggressive outlets of hockey and debating teams – the whole atmosphere that feeds my need for achievement and rewards me when I do achieve.

All this, however, simply covers the terrible mess I'm making of being me.

I share a room with my sister. My sister has a nervous habit. She sniffs. My father has the same nervous habit. He sniffs. He also has a nervous cough. I can't stand other people's twitching habits. Every time she sniffs I want to kill her. I want to smash her head in with my fists. But I can't very well do that so every time she sniffs I shout, 'Stop sniffing!' The fact that I shout at her every time she sniffs draws her attention to the fact that she sniffs and that makes her sniff all the more. I want to scream.

She also breathes. She goes to sleep sometimes before I do and then I can hear her breathing. I can't stand to hear her breathing so I shout out, 'Stop breathing so loudly!' She wakes up and cries and says she can't help breathing. I know she can't help breathing but I can't help the fact that I can't stand listening to her. When I hear her breathing a scream mounts up inside me, a monstrous, murderous rage and then I want to kill her. I'm not allowed to kill her so I go over and shake her. I make her roll over on to the other side. "Roll over,' I say, 'you're snoring.'

Apart from hating her, I also love her and we talk and giggle into the night. I do not remember what we talk about but I do remember the constant mother-cry, 'Off to sleep now,' followed ten minutes later by, 'That's quite enough talking for tonight.'

She if Fluffy and I am Bruno. We use our pet names for each other only at night, here, in the darkness of our room. She is the soft, white, cuddly rabbit and I am the big, strong, brown bear. I love my strength and display it constantly, like a muscle-man. I am Bruno, the bear, and she, dear little Fluffy rabbit, understands and in the friendship of the night lets me play my role.

I am compulsive about the number of times we must say good night. The number must be even. After five minutes of giggle and chatter I say, 'Good night, Fluffy.'

'Good night, Bruno.'

'Let's make some dolls' clothes tomorrow,' I add.

'Alright,' she sleepily, littler than I, replies.

'Good night, Fluffy.' She is almost asleep. 'I said, "Good night," Fluffy.'

She struggles back to wakefulness. 'Sorry, good night, Bruno.'

'Say it properly again,' I ask, 'to make it all even. Good night, Fluffy.'

'Good night, Bruno.' The ritual completed. I feel free to fall asleep.

She wins me often, this little soft rabbit, to her feminine pursuits. I play dolls with her and hospitals and mothers and fathers. I am always the father.

I long for her simplicity. She seems satisfied with pink and ribbons, frills and lace. I always want blue, unable to accept my fate.

She starts to outstrip me, to grow taller than I am, to overtake me and as she moves with surety towards her feminine role, even longing to become a woman, I creep backwards.

We fight a lot, this sister and I – bickering bitchiness of sisters. I am jealous of her because she is so slim and she's jealous of me because I have big tits. I wish she had them instead of me. I would sink, if I could, into a mound of mud, dissolve and disappear into the surface of the earth.

Yet the world of women intrigues me. I love nothing more than to sit with my mother and her friends and listen to them gossip. I hope that they will reveal to me the secret mysteries of women. I refuse to ask questions. I learn only by what I overhear and my knowledge is therefore confused and incomplete. She uses words like 'period', 'menstruation', 'becoming a woman' – which is correct? I don't know. I look up all the words with sexual connotations. Our big Webster's dictionary gives me a muddled assortment of facts. There is no taboo in my family about discussing such matters but the talk, like my mother, is scientific and unemotional. I know all about sperm and ovaries; I know nothing about love.

On my fourteenth birthday it begins. She's been threatening me for the last six months. 'I'll give you until you're fourteen,' she says, ' and then I'm going to see about you.' She takes me to a doctor. He's an endocrine specialist. He looks at me, weighs me, measures me. He examines the shape of my hands. 'She's not a cretin,' he says, looking at my mother. He looks some more. 'There's nothing wrong with her glands,' he adds.

'But don't you think she's too fat,' says my mother.

'I suppose she could go on a diet,' he replies. She leaves satisfied; I am bewildered. She has got what she came for. The Doctor-God has given his sanction to putting me on a diet. This she does with great enthusiasm. I am introduced to my life-long tormentor, the calorie. She is quite generous. She allows me 1,800 of them a day. She even permits me an ice cream cone each day, to be bought at the school canteen. I would like to please her. I would share her enthusiasm if I could, but I can't and I don't tell her about the sticky cream bun I feel compelled to buy each day.

Being put on a diet hurls me back in time. I am eight years old. I am standing in the kitchen with my brother and my sister. It is after-dinner-time and we are waiting, our little palms open, ready to receive the daily sweet ration. What will it be tonight? She takes out a packet of Jaffas and counts six little orange balls into each hand. No more. Total equality and no added indulgences. But I love sweets and need more than her allotment and every day I go to the shop across the road from out school and spend my pennies on lollies. Every night, in the bath, I confess to her, chant my sins of sweet buying and eating, and she cleanses me, absolves and washes me at the same time.

I am too big for confession now. The time for deception has arrived. The time has also arrived for me to become a thief. She deprives me and I will not be deprived. I become an early-morning riser. I get up at 5 am. I creep downstairs and raid the biscuit cupboard, the fridge, the bread bin. She always has lots of food. The trick is to steal enough to satisfy me but not so much that the theft is obvious. Does she count the biscuits she cooks? I don't know. Numbers become magical. I must take six, or ten, or twelve or twenty. Never odd numbers. I always start with six. Does the magic of this number lie in the six Jaffas or six Minties she used to dole out each night? Six is the number she considered adequate, fair but not over-indulgent. It is the limit she sets. So I try six first, but six is not enough for me so I take four more. That makes ten and ten is an attempt to set my own limit, a self-boundary. But I can't stay inside that boundary either. Another two will make twelve, a nice even number, another attempt to set up some self control. When that limit fails, the increase to twenty is like tearing down all fences. There is no hope left after twenty and even before I get to twenty I know there is no way I'll be able to stop because twenty biscuits or twenty lollies or twenty slices of bread and butter represent gluttony, piggish, revolting gluttony – in anyone's terms, even my own.

I spend all my pocket money on sweets. I like best to buy packets of chewy lollies – Fantales or Colombine Caramels. I like them because they last so long. I can lie in bed and eat them slowly in the middle of the night, lolly after lolly after lolly. I gobble them all up, no matter how sick and full I might feel. I do not know what physical hunger is. Often I eat so much that I have difficulty swinging myself off the bed. When I try to move the food fills my throat and pushes itself against the glands behind my ears. But I never vomit. I will not give it up. It's my food and I keep it safe inside me.

Once before I tried to hold on but she wouldn't let me. I was four years old and refused to shit. I held on to it for over a week and then she sent me to hospital and they gave me an anaesthetic and they took my shit away. She won't let me keep anything of my own. So I eat and eat and eat. It's the only way I know of holding on.

She finds other diets for me to go on; the hard-boiled egg and tomato diet, the bananas and milk diet, the meat and salad diet, the grapefruit diet, the six prunes for breakfast and one pound of meat for dinner diet. Her zeal and enthusiasm never flag.

She hears about a doctor who is experimenting with some new drug that is supposed to make children grow taller. It is not just my fatness that she finds unacceptable; my height is also less than adequate. So she takes me along to this nice doctor and he injects this drug into my backside twice a week for six months and we all wait for the miracle to happen. I even do stretching exercises up the wall each day to help the process along. After all, I don't want to be a freak. But there's no miracle for me and after six months he decides to have X-rays taken and the X-rays show that I stopped growing years ago and they've all wasted their time and I've had bruises on my bottom for six months for no reason at all.

And in the middle of all this is the terror of my parents. She sits with me on the stairs that lead to our bedrooms. She puts her arms around me. She bursts into tears. I've never seen her cry like this before. 'You're never going to grow any taller,' she says, blurting out her terrible news.

My father is distraught. 'It's my fault,' he says. 'It's all my fault. It's my side of the family that's short and fat.' I am dragged in by their neurosis. I weep with them. It is the end of the world. He comes to me that night. He is almost crying. He sits on my bed. He does not touch me. He sighs. 'Being little,' he says, 'either brings out the best or the worst in you. You need to make sure it brings out the best in you.' I start to cry but it is dark and I don't let him see my tears. I don't know whether I'm crying for him or for me. After all, he's little and he's done well and everyone likes him. Part of me doesn't understand what all this fuss is about. When he's gone I look out of my big window and watch the stars. I decide at that moment that there is no God. My decision is based on the fact that if there were a God I would hate him so it would be better if he didn't exist at all.

When I am sixteen she finds me another doctor. This one lives in Melbourne. He is experimenting with the use of high doses of thyroid for fatties. My mother and I go there for six weeks. She stays with friends and they put me into a hospital.

I don't mind being in hospital. In fact, I really like it. They starve me, allowing me only 600 calories a day but I don't mind being hungry. They have relieved me of the enormous burden of trying to exercise self control. The hospital is a prison, but it is also a guardian. I feel safe. And I am given the ultimate reward. I emerge butterfly-beautiful, tiny-slim. I love myself and they love me and I can't stop looking at myself in mirrors. At last I satisfy them. I am exactly what they want me to be. For a few months I purr and parade and thrive under their praise. I wear a bikini for the first time. I am no longer hidden under mounds of uncomfortable flesh. And then suddenly, compulsively, it begins again. I eat and eat. I cannot stop. Within two months I'm as fat as I was before. I do not understand.

She finds another doctor, this time in Sydney. He is experimenting with even more massive doses of thyroid. He introduces me to the magic of the diuretic that frees you of your fat by getting you to piss gallons of fluid each day. He puts me back into hospital and I want to go there as much as my parents want me to go. The image of the slim, tiny self taunts me. If I could just look like that again, stay like that, then surely some boy would love me, marry me. But it never works. I move in and out of hospital. I keep trying to recover self and failing. My body becomes like some great unstable bulge, constantly changing pattern and shape and form.

In the hospital I live from meal time to meal time. They have, very kindly, introduced me to the marvels of Dexedrine but, despite this drug, hunger is my constant companion. I examine hunger, live with an empty belly, an aching gut. It comes in waves that I must ride and I know that if I can get over the crest of one wave then there will be a period of respite, a time of repose when the gnawing in my gut is bearable. I hear the click of trays, smell the food. I feel the saliva rising in my mouth. My food has no smell. I am, by my own choice, on a starvation diet. All I will get is a lettuce leaf and a slice of tomato.

No one puts me in hospital now. I ask to go. No one says I must stick to 300 calories a day. I devise this torture for myself. No one says I must stay here for four weeks. I beg to be allowed to stay. I repeat the same pattern over and over again. I go to hospital; I get slim; I leave hospital; I eat; I get fat. And I am foolish enough to believe that each trip to hospital will be the last, stupid enough to think that surely this time the miracle will occur and I will stay slim and free forever.

But I love it here in hospital. I like to give up the struggle, to surrender to the arms of death. While others shrink in horror at the sight of concentration camp victims, I, alone, envy them. My ultimate fantasy is to be as thin as an Auschwitz survivor. That is my Paradise. Sometimes I imagine I might contract some dread disease, lie helpless for months in a coma and wake up so thin that I would have to be fed cream cakes and chocolate all day. Or maybe I could have a terrible car accident, be so smashed up that I will waste away, become light as a feather, have my bones stick out. It never happens. It never will. Situations that make other people thin, make me fat. If I'm worried, I eat; if I'm nervous, I eat; if I'm happy, I eat; if I'm sad, I eat. If the person closest to me died, I'd put on two stone. I will never reach Paradise.

Even now, here in the hospital, I cheat. It's a small, private hospital and I have a room to myself because I don't want to talk to anyone. I listen to the doctors having morning tea in a small area outside the operating theatre. I hear the cups of tea clinking on the saucers. When I think they're gone, I get up and pretend that I'm going to the toilet. I make sure no one sees me because I am terrified of being found out. I go past the morning tea area. Sometimes they've left one or two pieces of cake or buttered bun or pikelets. I snatch whatever is left and rush to the toilet, lock myself in and swallow down the spoils. Sometimes a nurse comes and takes the tray away before I get out there. When this happens I feel cheated. I feel worse than when I make it and find that the pigs have eaten all their morning tea and left none for me. The sight of the empty white plate appalls me.

I do not think of myself as a cheat or as a thief, because I am compelled to steal. It is not just food. I steal money as well. I steal money from my mother's purse to buy food. Even in hospital I make sure I have plenty of money. I go for walks and buy the newspaper to read, but this is only a trick because I buy lollies as well.

I have to be careful, though. I can't afford to be found out and I can't run the risk of putting on weight. After all, it's not humanly possible to put on weight on a diet of 300 calories a day. So this eating is only a little acting out, a token gesture of defiance. I don't do it every day. My cheating is the only expression of my life force. Apart from this I am inexpressibly weak, listless and dead.

My real binges are saved for my release, when there's no one to stop me, no scales to check my weight, no one to construct the barriers of control that I am quite incapable of erecting from within myself.

Normality is no longer possible. It is too late. I fill my cup-boards and drawers with empty packet of lolly papers. I'm afraid to throw them away in case my mother sees them in the rubbish bin. I'm also afraid of her finding them in my room. I stuff them behind my clothes. I sometimes do the same with used sanitary pads – wrap them up and stuff them in with my underclothes. I don't know why I do it.

The plane jerks to a rough landing. The airport. Amsterdam. I am more shocked by the past than by the present. I am horrified by the hospitals. The pink snake lady wriggles across my path. Her hard, cold face smirks at me. I can't cope. The plane oppresses me. I am locked in, claustrophobic womb. What am I to do?

A pleasant female voice tells us that transit passengers are to remain on the plane, informs us that health regulations require that the plane must be fumigated, warns us that if we are allergic to aerosol sprays we should cover our faces with a handkerchief. Thank you very much for your co-operation, ladies and gentlemen. We trust that those passengers who are leaving the plane at Amsterdam had a pleasant trip. Thank you for flying Qantas. Do travel with us again.

I recover myself. I look around the plane. The people are exhausted now. No one cares what they look like, no pretence of enjoyment, no sense of adventure or excitement. Everyone feels dirty, no one gives a damn. I look at the strained faces of parents with small children. The children are crying now – intolerable, tired tears. How glad I am that my babies are safely home, not here with me.

We sit for one hour, waiting. This is normal. We are not aware that anything is wrong until the cheery Captain's voice comes over the PA system: 'Ladies and gentlemen, we are sorry but there is a small delay. Fog at London airport. Have to wait for it to clear. You can disembark. We'll give you a voucher for a free drink. Stay close to gate 21. We'll let you know as soon as we are ready to take off.'

I smile to myself. I'm glad we're delayed. I long to stretch my legs. It's nine o'clock in the morning.

I walk up and down. Strange people, strange sounds, different languages, bright lights, signs, smiles, miles of moving footways.

'Sorry,' says the pleasant, Amsterdam-trained Qantas man, 'the fog is very bad…can't take off … can't land … don't know how long … just as soon as we know … will let you know.'

I walk again. I trek up and down, up and down, up and down, dragging my exhausted body with me. Is it possible to get through the fog, throw off the past, walk one's way to freedom? I try. I do try. And then I give up. I sit down, make a pillow of my coat, put my legs on the seat and let myself drift and dream.

I am fourteen years old and I am going to my first party. I feel excited about going. I don't quite know what to expect. I'm wearing a bra and stockings. I make sure the seams are straight. I hate wearing stockings because they pull across my plump thighs. The weight of the stockings seems to pull at the suspender belt until my stockings sag. I feel as if I have to keep hitching them up. I wear lipstick for the first time. It feels peculiar on my lips. I don't like its taste and it makes me feel as if I can't talk naturally.

The party is being given by a girl in the year above me at school. I am invited because we are all in the same Jewish scripture class and we all belong to the same Jewish Youth Clubs and, above all, because I have an eligible big brother. I arrive at the party with my brother, two male cousins and the boy next door. How lucky and secure I must seem to the girls who arrive alone.

At Jewish Youth Club dances my brother often chooses me as his partner. He swirls me round in a magic waltz and no moments are more precious to me than the moments I spend spinning in his arms. The younger of my male cousins also dances with me but I feel no pride when he does. He is afraid of the girls and feels safe with me. It saves him from venturing forth and trying himself out. It saves me too. I don't have to worry about being a wallflower. On the other hand, he dances with me so much that no one else can dance with me, even if they wanted to. Mostly I'm grateful that he is there but sometimes I wish he would disappear.

I am dancing with him now. We are outside because it is a very warm night. I look over towards the dark shadows of the fence. I look and look again. My eyes cannot believe what they are seeing. There is a girl there. She is standing with a boy and they are kissing. I am so shocked that I keep looking and looking. No one else seems to be shocked although I notice that everyone is very curious.

We have supper inside, with the lights on. Cakes and pavlovas, fruit salad and ice cream. Soft drinks, of course. After supper a conversation begins about kissing. The girl I had seen outside starts the conversation. Her sexual precocity still leaves me shattered but it is as if she is trying to liberate us, to set us off on the road to sexuality.

'Have you ever kissed anyone,' she asks me. She is ignoring the boys. She has a small group of girls around her.

'No,' I say.

'Do you want to try?'

I want to say 'No' but she's being friendly and I don't like to refuse. 'Alright,' I say. She puts her hands on my cheeks and she kisses me. It feels strange, but not unpleasant. Our teeth touch. 'Why do our teeth touch,' I want to know.

'That often happens,' she laughs, sensuously. 'You have to practise.' She kisses me again. Then we girls all start kissing each other and giggling. We experiment. We touch tongues.

'Stop it,' my brother says. He's embarrassed. I can't see why. We are just having fun and what is fun is that we totally exclude the boys from our fun. I would like to try kissing my brother. I suggest this to him and he turns away from me in horror. But my cousin doesn't turn away. He says he'd like to try it and we kiss each other.

I go home feeling very strange. I have the vague feeling that I've done something wrong.

I start to look forward to the next party. I go to it and a boy, who is not my cousin, dances with me. They turn off the lights and put on Charles Trenet singing 'La Mer'. They play it over and over again and I dance softly, cheek to cheek, for the first time.

And now my life of fantasy begins. My brother has a very handsome friend and I imagine myself to be in love with him. He never notices me but every night, in my imaginings, he and I run towards each other on Bondi beach. He runs from one end of the beach and I run from the other. We run in slow and graceful motion. We meet at the exact centre of the beach, locked in eternal embrace. We kiss in ecstasy. I know nothing about sex. I do not even know that it exists. I know that sperm from the male fertilizes eggs from the female but I have no idea of the process by which such a thing happens. But in the fantasy of the kiss I can feel that the kiss is not enough. I imagine the kiss; I live the kiss and my insides tell me that there must be something else, but my mind cannot imagine what that something else might be.

People start to pair themselves off, to become couples, to choose each other as experimental mates. No one chooses me. My sister, at twelve, meets the boy she will, in fact, later marry. My brother takes out an endless stream of pretty Jewish girls. No one wants me. My cousin continues to look after me. No one wants him, either. We are like a lame, odd, outcast pair. I am always looking at other people holding hands. There is no one to hold mine. It is terrible to be fourteen, fifteen, sixteen and to watch those around you, in your closed circle of friends, arrange and re-arrange themselves into closely coupled pairs – to be one the girls that no boy chooses.

Because I am not chosen, I become, in my own eyes, all the more undesirable. I start to opt out, withdraw, refuse to go any-where. I no longer wear make-up. I refuse to follow the pattern of other girls. Their faces, like my mother's, with rouged cheeks and red lips, repel me. Their masks are a parody of femininity. I cannot be part of it. I stand alone, telling myself that if I cannot be loved for what I am then I do not want to be loved at all. And I am not loved – not at all. I kiss my own image in the mirror because there's no one else to kiss.

Both my brother and my sister are looking outside the family. I am totally turned within. Both he and she have their other life. I have only them.

The three of us become friends. Having battled our way through childhood, we become a harmonious threesome. We often sit up all night talking about God, eternity, morality, the stars; our parents, our future, our hopes, our desires, our fears. We explore each other's intellects. We solve the problems of the world.

We walk, sometimes, this brother and I, along the cliffs that are near our home. He tries to give me the sense of wonder he feels at the splendour of the natural world around him. He writes reams of verse but never shows it to anyone. His poetic soul floods and warms me. I bask in his light. I feel that we are so alike, he and I, and I truly follow him in all he does. I look up to him, worship him, long for his love. He hurts me because he is only interested in taking out beautiful girls. Why is he so shallow? Why can't he see that he should be looking for a girl like me – someone who could be his soulmate, his friend, an ever ready vessel into which he could pour his thoughts and his feelings, his hopes and his despair. I feel that he slaps me in the face. I am not worthy of his love.

We share a love of music and we lie for hours on the lounge room floor, brim full of Dvorjak, Beethoven and Sibelius. When he is out, I lie there alone with our music, lost in romantic reverie of the handsome boy who will love me for what I am and whisk me away to live happily ever after. My Knight in Shining Armour. I wait for him still.

Sexless, sterile years. I do not masturbate. I don't explore my body. I have no secret box, no warm cunt, no dark womb. I have only my lion, with his rumbling, mountainous roar.

The prospect of leaving school terrifies me. I am safe there. At school I can escape. I can play hockey, debate, achieve. Now I have to choose a career. I would like to do an Arts Degree but my mother tells me that I cannot do this unless I am prepared to become a teacher. I know that I could never be a teacher so I have to make a different choice. I am such a poor excuse for an individual that I choose my mother's career and decide to become a pharmacist. Perhaps I feel that this will please her. I would like to please her and I would like to be a good girl. If I'm a good girl and if I please her then perhaps she will learn to love me.

She finds an apprenticeship for me and I start to work in a chemist shop. The man I am apprenticed to is a soft, gentle Jew, genuinely helpful, wanting to teach me all he knows. I love to work for him but within a few months he sells out to a brassy Jew who doesn't give a damn about me and is just out to make as much as he can. He doesn't teach me anything and I start to feel like a slave. The real world is getting too difficult for me to handle.

Something really scary happens to me now. My weight starts to escalate. Until now I have always fluctuated within set limits – seven stone at the lowest, nine and a half stone at the highest. Now it goes up and up. Ten stone; ten and a half stone; eleven stone; eleven and a half stone. I am a real thief now. I earn money but nowhere near enough to satisfy my compulsive need for food. The chemist shop sells sweets – blocks of chocolate and glucose jelly beans. I steal these but I also steal money from the till and food from other shops. I live in terror of being found out.

This is not like stealing food at home. I am committing real crimes punishable by law and I can't help it. My need for food is so overwhelming that I cannot find any way of controlling my actions. I balloon. People stare at me in the street. I waddle. I steal little bottles of sweet cascara and shit myself empty in some helpless attempt to evacuate the enormous quantities of food I'm consuming.

By the end of six months my breakdown is complete. I beg to return to hospital, telling my mother that this will definitely be the last time, the last trip. I want to be my seven stone self and I'll never, never, never ask to go back to hospital again. I am begging now, pleading with her to give me this last chance. She goes to work now and it costs the whole of her salary each week to keep me in hospital. She sees how desperate I am. She has to agree. She must be as terrified as I am of this monstrous, waddling, ugly freak. She is relieved, I think, to have me safely away again.

I am so afraid of messing it all up that I choose a different hospital this time. I can't trust myself in the other place, can't go through the daily temptation of plotting to steal the doctors' leftover crumbs. There are to be no loopholes this time. I think the new hospital will provide me with the security I so desperately need to harness myself back into an acceptable form.

I make new rules – I am not to be permitted to leave the hospital grounds. I construct a Spartan diet – 300 calories a day. The diet calls for one, big, perfect apple each day. I tell my mother that I don't trust the hospital to buy good apples and I ask her to bring me one when she visits me each night. I dream all day of the apple she will bring me, long to sink my teeth into its hard crispness – this symbol of love that I force her to give me each and every day of my imprisonment.

It takes me six months to lose the required four and a half stone. For six months I do not see the sun or feel the wind or touch the earth. I do not leave my room. I atone for my sins with the daily agony of hunger. I become incredibly weak. I do not exercise. It takes one hour of total rest to recover from my daily bath. I live an extraordinary existence. I'm never bored. I listen to radio. I read books. I long for the next meagre meal. I dream of the apple that my mother will bring me. I float on a Dexedrine high, fall artificially asleep with the help of sleeping pills. Every second day I am injected with diuretics. The constant loss of fluid makes me dizzy and weak but I don't mind. I am flirting with death.

I sit up in Amsterdam airport. I sit up and despite all the people around me, the tears pour down my face. I start to sob and sob and even now, while I am trying to write about sitting up in Amsterdam airport – even now the tears flood and my body shakes and my pen quivers and my writing becomes an unreadable scrawl as I cry my loneliness to the empty air because I don't know, even now, I don't know what the hell I was doing there, dying there, loving the dying, longing to go on dying in a sterile, empty room.

For they are all the same, aren't they, all those hospital rooms? I am only ever four months old, aren't I? Hungry, afraid and almost dead, longing, longing, longing for warm mother arms. Four months or forty years – I long for them still. To be rocked, to be cradled, to be held. For if one has never known the soft-breast, the warm-suck, the earth-flow, the mother-giving; if one has always longed and never received, then the other thing, the darkness, the cavern, the death-womb beckons and calls, tempting, alluring, enticing, inviting, offering oblivion, sweet surrender, the peaceful promise of the dead.

I struggle with my hysteria. I am saved by a voice over the loudspeaker announcing that we cannot leave Amsterdam. It is now 6 pm and we are to be taken to a hotel for the night. I am nothing now. I have ceased to exist. I merge with the crowd, becoming just one of the 405 people who are to be taken by bus to a hotel in Amsterdam. We arrive; we are given splendid rooms; we are fed. I don't dare to talk to anyone. I creep into the darkness of the warm hotel bed and curl myself to sleep. Hotel. Hospital. I sink into the womb.

FOUR

Thirteen hours of sleep stitch me together again, patch me, mend me, sew me up so that no one would ever know that I'd split my seams and fallen apart. Eros wins again, hurls Thanatos down and sends his victory cry flying through my veins.

Amsterdam to London. I take my seat on the plane to the accompaniment of the more than familiar take-off routine – orange juice, wet towels, life-saving drill, the friendly patter over the PA system. I'm an old hand now. I slip into jet travel as if I'd never done anything else.

Take-off. One hour to go – no further than a trip from Sydney to Melbourne. Melbourne – I only need to sit back and close my eyes and I am there. I am eighteen years old. Coming to Melbourne is important because it represents my one and only adolescent grasp for independence. It is the year following the long year of the hospital. It is the year for thinking and searching; it is the year for growing up; it is the year for making decisions and I, in my eighteen-year-old wisdom, have decided to become a dietitian. It is logical, isn't it, that if you have a particular problem then you want to learn all you can about it. You pretend to yourself that you want to cure and help others; what you really want is to cure and help yourself. You enter your profession in the guise of the saviour, in the desperate hope that the soul you save will be your own. A compulsive eater would make a very bad dietitian but I don't know that.

They are glad about my decision, this family of mine. So eager are they for me to achieve, to undertake some course of action of which they can approve, that they jump with delight at my suggestion. Perhaps, indeed, they are heartily sick of me. How unpleasant it must be to see my failure constantly parading before their eyes.

My parents have a friend in Melbourne and I am to go to her place every Friday night for dinner so that I will not forget that I am a Jew and so that I will feel that I have a warm and loving home away from home. I have met this family before and I like them very much. She is, as far as I can see, an extraordinary mother. She has one grown-up son of nineteen and, from her second marriage, a small daughter of two. She is stepmother to an older boy who comes from her husband's first marriage. But it is not in the area of her own family unit that her motherliness impresses me; it is in the way she allows her mother-arms and her mother-love to extend to all those who she sees orphaned around her. She is a survivor of Nazi concentration camps and after the war she helped orphaned Jewish boys to escape Europe and come to a new life in Australia. Those of her boys who live in Melbourne see her still as the Mother, the Saviour and each Friday night her home is open and her hospitality flows to all who are in need of warmth and food and love. I look forward to my Friday night visits.

I am to stay at Women's College, just outside the University grounds. I meet my room-mate. She is a bright, lively girl from Tasmania. She is doing a course to become a Physical Education teacher and we are as different from each other as it is possible for two girls to be. But we get along well and, during these first few weeks, we lie in the dark, talking for hours, smoking cigarettes, a newly acquired habit that seems suitable to our grown-up, away-from-home independence. She is worldly wise and I'm a baby. She knows all about boys and I know nothing. We get high on cigarette smoke and allow ourselves to float dizzily to sleep.

I love college life. I like being in an institution. Discipline is not difficult and there is always someone to talk to. Especially

I like college food. I like it because it's starchy and stodgy and because there are always desserts. I like it because if I have a piece of toast for breakfast no one stares at me with disapproval. And because no one stares at me with disapproval I only need to eat one piece. It's not wrong to eat trifle or baked custard. Everyone eats it. It's not even wrong to put on weight. It happens to everyone. So I'm just like everyone else for the first time. No one thinks that I'm a freak.

I go to the house of the Good Mother and, if I let myself, I can still recapture the feeling of that first Friday night visit. I enter the house through the back way, by means of the kitchen. I see the little two-year-old sitting in her high chair. I walk in, ready to greet the child with a smile. Suddenly I stop. A man is bending down beside the high chair, talking to the little girl. There is no one else in the room. He looks up and I stare at him. He is the handsomest man I've ever seen. He has deep olive skin, black slightly curling hair, large brown-black eyes, perfect features set in a high cheek-boned, oval face. My insides seize. I catch my breath. I fall in love in an instant. I don't know who he is but I know immediately that I will love him forever.

The lady of the house comes into the kitchen, smiling Jewish mother, kissing me. She introduces me to the man. He is one of her orphan boys.

And now I long for Friday nights, not for the family warmth they provide, but to be again in the presence of the man I love. I spend my entire waking time dwelling in the fantasy of loving and marrying him. I cannot concentrate on my classes at the university. My mind is not attuned to physics and chemistry and biology and botany. Science bewilders me and I allow myself to remain bewildered. All that matters is my inner life, my fantasies. I lose myself in love.

All the big brothers who I meet on Friday nights become my friends. They take me to Jewish Youth Clubs, to picnics, on outings. It seems to me that Melbourne Jews are more hospitable than their Sydney counterparts and I respond to the real warmth and generosity that I feel flowing from these people.

He, the object of my love, becomes my friend. He lives alone in a flat just near the university. He always has time for me. We talk and talk. I become his little sister. He loves beautiful women and has lots of girlfriends. He is so handsome that women are always chasing him. But me – little, plain, plump me – I am his sister and his friend. I spend weekends at his flat. I sleep on the lounge. I would give anything in the world to sleep in his bed, to kiss him, to lie warm and still by his side.

All his family are dead, killed during the war. My family are in Sydney and it is as if they are dead to me. We become each other's family. My secret life is the fantasy that one day he will realize that beauty in women is unimportant. One day he will look at his little sister-friend in a new light. With wonder and amazement he will gaze into my face and know that I am the woman he really loves.

Although I go along to Jewish Youth functions I find that the same thing happens to me as happened to me in Sydney. Everyone likes me but no one asks me out. I still don't correspond to the average Jewish boy's idea of beauty but, in Melbourne, I don't seem to feel so bad about it. I don't have my brother and my cousin to support me but I have all these substitute big brothers and I never really feel lonely. Besides, there is the reality of the dream world I inhabit. I am quite sure that the man I love will marry me one day – look after me and love me and give me beautiful babies. Fantasy feeds upon fantasy, dream upon dream of wedded and domestic bliss. It is sufficient. I am sustained.

I go home for the May holidays. What hurts me is that they are all managing so well without me. In fact, I sense that it is much more peaceful for everyone else in the family when I am not around. My brother has his girlfriend, my sister has her boyfriend and I feel strangely alienated. Within a few days of my arrival the girl who will one day be my sister-in-law says to me, 'It's so strange to have you home again. I'm so used to there being just the four of us.' Her comment sends me flying back to Melbourne the next day.

It is winter now and I long for Sydney. It's so much colder here and I have chilblains all over my toes even though I wear fur-lined boots. I contract bronchitis and feel dreadfully ill. My temperature is so high that I am floating but it's Friday night and I must get to my substitute family's home, must not lose the opportunity of seeing my loved one's dark, sensuous face. He has a habit of playing with hair, twirling small pieces of it into twisted curls with his fingers. How I long just to touch the smoothness of his skin. I have never touched his skin but I know that it would melt into mine. My lips ache to touch his lips, my hand to touch his hand. Each time I see him the spasm stabs inside me, the longing for just one kiss. Can't he see that I'm in love with him? No. I'm the little sister-friend. He loves me but not in the way that I long to be loved.

The Jewish mother sees how ill I am and insists on putting me to bed. The doctor is called and pneumonia is diagnosed and she, good mother, looks after me. My own mother flies down from Sydney to see me and, as I later learn, she pays the Jewish mother to be a mother to me.

This woman wins me. I am easily seduced, a willing victim to good mothering. She suggests that I should live with her and makes an arrangement with my parents so that they now pay her instead of paying the college. I fall into her trap. She really just wants the generous amount of money my parents send her each week. She does not care about me. Gradually I learn that, sugar-sweet outside, she is vicious and destructive within. She is the praying mantis who eats her mate. She creates tension between son and stepson, son and stepfather, father and son. She, queen bee, centre of all things, feeds on us all. I am lost in the smothering breast.

It is suddenly October and the year is drawing to a close. The prospect of impending examinations does not frighten me. I do not even begin to study. I think I have always known that I would never sit for them. That realization is coupled with an acceptance that I must go home. If I am going to drop out of university then there is no logical reason for my remaining in Melbourne. Failure descends upon me. I have allowed myself to be swallowed up. I have not found myself. My bid for independence has been unsuccessful. Instead I have allowed the mother arms to smother, suffocate, destroy.

I make one final effort to assert my individuality before I leave. I make a determined, conscious decision to lose my virginity.

I go, with a Jewish girlfriend, to a non-Jewish party. Actually, it's a Communist party. People who've been to Russia get up and give little speeches about brotherhood. It's all beyond me. I have no idea what they're talking about. Everyone is friendly and it's very different from a Jewish party. I have anonymity here. No one knows who I am or where I come from or what my father does or how much he earns. No one gives a damn.

A handsome Northern Greek wharf labourer takes a fancy to me. He talks to me all night, dances with me, chats me up. He wants to take me home. Though I'm very naïve and innocent, I do know enough to realize that he intends to take me home to his place and to his bed.

I make the decision to go with him. My friend asks, 'Do you know what you are doing?'

'I want to lose my virginity,' I reply, 'and it might just as well be with him.' He has been kissing me at the party. His tongue thrusts its way into my mouth, half-way down my throat. I've never been kissed like this before. I know exactly what I'm doing.

He takes me home. His room is shabby, small, poor, dilapidated – quite outside my middle-class experience. He has a red, coloured globe in his bedside table lamp. This is the only light he allows in the room. It is eerie and frightening and my heart is pounding in my throat. He goes to the toilet.

'Get into bed,' he says. I undress quickly and get into bed. I leave my pants on. He comes back and gets in beside me. It is a single, narrow bed. He feels my pants. 'What's this for?' he asks. 'Take them off.'

'I'm a virgin,' I reply, as I remove my pants. He laughs at me. He doesn't believe me. I can see that, as far as he is concerned, there are no virgins left in Melbourne.

'You don't kiss like a virgin,' he says. My apprehension rises and, for a moment, I wish that I were anywhere else in the world except here in this ugly room. I feel something hard and hot next to my leg and I don't know what it is. He takes my hand and guides it so that I can feel the full vigour of his maleness. The encyclopaedias I've read have told me nothing at all about this. I am filled with a sense of wonder and yet my moment of surprise is also a moment of recognition as if I have, at last, come face to face with a truth I have always known.

Suddenly he is lying on top of me and I would like to cry out "Leave me alone!' but I cannot make myself say the words. I would like to believe that the reason I cannot say the words is that I am terrified, shocked dumb. But that would be a lie. The reason that I do not scream is that I do not want to scream. There is a terrible, dark part of me that welcomes what is happening; there is within me a pulsating blackness that longs to be stabbed and torn, mutilated and raped. And though a small part of me resists, I know that he is doing to me the very thing that I want to be done.

It is difficult for him to enter me and, instinctively, my body becomes taut and rigid and I close myself up to lock him out but he won't be locked out. And then I just lie there and let it happen and I feel him burn and stab and sear into me and then thrust and pound and batter me until it's over and he's finished with me. Then he rolls off me and he moves me aside and he sees the blood and he cries, 'Shit! I'm sorry! Forgive me, I'm sorry!' but I can't answer him. I stumble out bed and I'm shaking so badly that my hands can hardly hold my pants as I try to dress myself. I think he's torn my insides apart and drops of blood and sperm trickle down my legs. My thighs are like jelly as I rush out into the street and hail a taxi to take me home. As I curl into bed I feel like a wounded puppy, hurt and confused. I am somewhat bewildered by the strange sense of joy that accompanies my pain.

I never want to see him again but, somehow, he finds me. He feels guilty and he wants to undo the damage he thinks he's done to me. The day before I am to leave for Sydney he rents a room in a hotel and we stay there for a day and a night and he tries, in every way he knows, to teach me the gentleness and the beauty of love. I fail. I like the softness of his touch, the warmth of his caresses but there is no orgasm for me. He thinks he's made me frigid but can I really blame him? I think not. It is I who am to blame for I have never touched, never explored, never allowed myself to find the sexual pleasure of self. It is I who see my body as ugly. I – sexless, sterile.

We walk that night down by the Melbourne wharves. He says he hopes I'll be alright. We lie down on the wharf and look at the stars. It is a warm, still, summer night. I look into his handsome face.

'If you put your hands around my throat,' he says, 'and strangled me, I would go on smiling at you and die happily.' What he has said is strange but I understand. The struggle between us is over. For the first time I lie quiet and calm in the arms of a man and I feel total peace. I am the conquered, gazing serenely into the eyes of my destroyer.

I stir in my seat, feel the outlines of my body, aware that, at the moment, my body is reasonably small and I fit snugly into my jeans. As we approach Heathrow I purr to myself – no longer the frigid adolescent but a woman now of powerful sexuality, forty years old and in my prime, ready suddenly for adventure and excitement in the big, wide world. And I will not lose this time.

FIVE

London. It is ten o'clock in the morning as I make my slow way from one end of the plane to the other. I don't even mind that it is taking me so long to get off the plane. Nothing matters. I am inwardly confident and self-assured. I feel hot. I am wearing a jumper, carrying a heavy sheepskin coat and a crammed overnight bag. I expect to be hit with the London cold as soon as I leave the plane.

I join the passport queue for Commonwealth people. The queue seems eternal. I look at it with apprehension. It is barely moving. People around me become short-tempered but I click off and ignore them. I just stare at the people around me. I am fascinated by a small group next to me. I can't keep my eyes off them. There is one man and three old ladies and they look as if they are Indians. The women are wearing saris, woolly cardigans, socks and sandals. The man carries nothing but the women are each carrying two heavy plastic containers. They seem so primitive to me. They do not look anywhere, these women, but follow the man, their eyes cast down.

A rather fat and jolly Pakistani, who speaks excellent English, is behind me. He jokes and smiles about the long queues and laughingly estimates that it will take us at least one more hour to get through the passport check. He starts to talk to the Indian man and they converse in a foreign language for quite some time. When they have finished I am so curious that I ask him to tell me about the group. He tells me that the man is a priest and that he has just been back to India and that he is bringing the old ladies of his family to England for a holiday. The plastic containers are filled with holy water from the

Ganges. I decide that hours spent at airports cannot possibly be regarded as wasted.

I pass through the passport check and follow the signs that tell me where to collect my luggage and my body waits another hour while my eyes constantly watch the revolving suitcases, alert for the moment mine will appear.

When my suitcase arrives, I realize, quite unexpectedly, that I can't manage. There is no hope of finding a porter or a luggage trolley. I must walk and walk with my heavy suitcase, my overnight bag, my purse over one shoulder, my heavy coat. What I have to do seems to me an impossible physical task and yet I do it because there's no one to do it for me. The joys of independence seem far away as I struggle under the burden of being on my own. Somehow, I make it to the bus.

Too soon we arrive at Victoria Station. I don't want to arrive because I know I'm going to have to struggle with the luggage again. My left hand is now blistered and sore but, somehow, I make it to the taxi stand. I wait for a long time and finally get a cab and give the address of my hotel. It is only a short trip and I arrive to be met with politeness, concern and a man who actually carries my suitcase the sixty-five steps up to my room.

And now, this first week in London, I experience something I have longed for but never believed I would ever find – I become my eyes, instead of my mouth. I become a sponge, but a visual rather than an oral sponge. I take in, take in, take in, but not food. The hotel provides me with a solid English breakfast and I eat a meal at night because by then I'm starving but apart from that I'm too busy to eat.

It is my legs that have become compulsive. They must walk and walk and walk. For six or seven hours a day I walk the streets of London, endlessly looking. I am never cold. It is late

December but I don't need long underwear, not even a jumper – just jeans and thin cotton shirt and my warm coat. Everyone can tell I'm a tourist because I peel off my coat as soon as I get into the tube. Perhaps it is my constant movement, my enormous excitement that keeps me warm. I cannot tolerate the insides of buildings. The central heating oppresses me. Except for the insides of theatres. These I haunt. After three days I haven't set eyes on Westminster Abbey or Buckingham Palace but I've seen five plays. And the parks! I cannot believe the beauty and the size of the parks, the abundance and variety of the birds. Grey skies do not depress me here. It is hard, at first, to realize that, in London, grey skies do not mean rain. And where is the famous London rain? I begin to think I'm magic. People say things like, 'You should have been here two weeks ago. The weather was terrible, so cold you couldn't go outside.' I don't believe them. London is not cold and it never, never rains.

After a week I long to look outside of London and I take day trips to Salisbury and Stonehenge, to Oxford and Cambridge, to Brighton and Rye and to Stratford-upon-Avon where I go, in the dark of night, to Shakespeare's house and touch the walls and feel his spirit creeping into me. Wherever I go, I avoid guides. If I hear them talking to groups of people I refuse to listen. I want only to feel in my own way, at my own pace, in my own time.

I cannot sleep. My mind is reeling. Even in bed I am walking, walking, constantly propelled. I am too impatient to sleep. I long for morning so that I can start again.

What is so extraordinary to me is that each day is mine. And I do so many things in one day that the time does not go quickly. I savour and enjoy every moment. Each day seems like a week. What a contrast to getting up, making breakfast, getting the kids ready for school, going to work, coming home, making dinner, doing the washing, putting the kids to bed, going to sleep.

I spend most of my time alone but my friend, who lives in Perth, is also here in London with her ten-year-old son. We meet for dinner or to go to the theatre. Sometimes we spend the day together. I like the contact, the opportunity to talk about what is happening, or what is exciting. She and I are in tune. We respond in the same way to things around us. I enjoy her son because he is not my responsibility yet he constantly keeps my children in mind. He longs to know each of the four of them as people and keeps asking me how this one or that one would respond to what we see. Soon he knows them so well that he no longer asks but rather tells me how each would react to a particular place or circumstance, what each would think of the play we have just seen or the meal we have just eaten. My friend and I have a true friendship, a feeling for each other's needs. And because we see so little of each other in Australia, there is the very real pleasure that we gain from each other's company. We are sisters, she and I, and on this first voyage into the outer world we can find, in each other, momentary assurance, warmth and support.

But my need, primarily, is for aloneness and it is this that I delight in. I had thought that an overseas trip would be studded with exciting sexual encounters. This is a new and liberating experience for me, not just the realization that I am surviving alone but the deeply satisfying feeling that I prefer to be alone.

I am walking in Regent's Park. It is a crisp, sunny day and I long just to walk the hours away. A man comes up beside me. He starts talking to me; I don't really want to talk to him. He keeps walking with me; I don't really want to walk with him.

He is trying to pick me up; I don't really want to be picked up. In the end I talk to him because he is so persistent. I learn that he comes from Iran and that he, and two of his brothers, own a food shop in London. After talking to me and walking with me for a while he takes out £100 in notes and offers it to me if I will go home with him for just half an hour.

I laugh with real joy, feeling how satisfying it is to have been given some idea of my monetary worth. He is a nice man and when he is quite sure that I will not take up the offer he gives up and leaves me alone.

A few days later I am walking around Piccadilly Circus. I have a ticket to see a Brecht play but it's two hours before the play is due to begin. I feel tired but it's not worth going back to my hotel and I don't quite know what to do with myself. A man stops me and asks me if I would like to have a cup of coffee with him.

Every day something like this happens. Mostly I am polite, smile, say 'No thank you' and walk on. I look at him. He is copper brown and slim, beautifully dressed in deep chocolate colours. I make the judgment that he looks nice. I am momentarily aware of how frightened I am to make such a judgment. I am always wary and realize the danger of making the wrong decision. What if I am bashed over the head, robbed, have my passport and traveller's cheques stolen? I have developed the tourist's paranoid neurosis about my passport and money. They are always safely zippered in a special compartment in my shoulder bag. I walk always with my hand covering this pocket. I realize, of course, that I could still be knocked down and my bag stolen but it is not possible for a pickpocket to steal my valuables. Anyway, I decide that he looks safe and I feel like a cup of coffee and so I say 'Yes'.

We go to a coffee shop and we drink coffee and talk. Suddenly we are communicating. He is a civil engineer from Ceylon. We start to talk about being oneself and I know from what he says that he is not as free as I am. I become aware, as I have so many times before, that teaching is such an easy way of opting out of the materialistic, cut-throat world. I am able to live in my own select, insulated, little world that is both pleasant and intellectually satisfying. I no longer need a social face to put on to meet others in a false situation.

I can see that this man envies me. He must behave in particular ways to please his boss, his clients, the men who work for him. His life has become a series of roles and he longs for me because he feels that he might, momentarily, take over my freedom to be myself. He is doing me good. It is always satisfying to feel that one is freer than some other human being – especially if one is a woman, and the mother of four children.

We go to a pub and I am really grateful to him for taking me there because I am too shy to go into one alone and this is my first experience of a London pub. I really start to enjoy myself. I look down at my clothes and realize how little I do care about appearance. I wear my jeans all the time in London. Perhaps it is this that he likes about me. I give a lot; I encourage him; I try to tell him that not caring what other people think about you is a difficult thing to achieve. You have to work at it. Perhaps I want to teach him something; perhaps I wish to convince myself of the truth of what I'm saying.

And then he has to spoil it all by wanting me to go to bed with him. I have my ticket for the theatre and Brecht is the more important so I suggest that I meet him the next night. But he is insistent. He wants me now, this night. I think he is afraid that if he lets me go I will not come back. He is probably right. I want to say 'No'. That is the answer that it feels right to me to give. I do not want to go to bed with him. It would be wrong for me. But I have a long history of 'Yeses.' And so I say 'Yes' although I hate myself for giving in and we go home to his place and while I'm having a bath he goes out and buys a Chinese meal and we eat and drink and then he makes love to me. He is a good lover and he does all he can to try to satisfy me but it is as if I am outside myself and watching myself and my body is unresponsive, cold and uninvolved, frigid and unfeeling. By the time he has finished it is very late and I am not angry but I am filled with depression and despair. Moreover, I feel that he has trapped me and I am a prisoner in a jail, lying here beside him, because it is 2 am and the tube will not start running again until 5 am and I'm too afraid to go down and out into the streets at this time of night.

And so I have to stay here, waiting for the night to end. He goes to sleep. Before he does he tells me that he always sleeps with the light on.

As I lie here, caught, in this claustrophobic room, I go back to the many nights that I have spent, trapped in the same way, beside the man, my husband. Husband – still unfaced. No longer with me, always with me. Do I dare now to look and to uncover, to see and to understand? Must we travel always together? Or can I somehow undertake our painful dissection. And does the truth set one free? My thirteen-year mate – husband-father-mother-child-companion-friend. He was afraid of the dark – always a night light shining outside our room so that the people in the cupboards could not come out during the night to harm him. We squeezed each other's pimples and farted in each other's company – an ultimate measure of our intimacy.

I was twenty when we met. He was nineteen. We met at a Jewish Youth Camp – a terrible irony for we had both given up our faith. No satisfaction for me until this boy, virginal, passionate, longing, came to me. And I, virginal in spirit, emotion and response. We kissed, endlessly. Thick warm lips, dark smooth skin, dark curly hair, soft, soft skin. We kissed, touched, wanted, longed, had each other – in the old Holden car, at Coogee Beach, Ben Buckler, Neilsen Park – all the old lovers' haunts. Steaming up the windows. Stripped. So used to a car door to bash against that our first effort in a bed left us hopeless, helpless, laughing. Children both, seeking in each other some warmth and meaning, security and love. Shaky saplings, twined in mutual support.

I was the stronger one, when it all began. After Melbourne failure I'd been given another chance. I was doing my second year of an Arts Degree and I was doing well. He'd opted out after one year of a psychology course. He was a stammerer and could barely get out a word without faltering. But he was clever and handsome, loving and warm and I didn't mind about his stammer. I was ten and a half stone and fat and he didn't mind about my being fat. I'm lying. I did mind about his stammer. I hated it. It embarrassed me. It wasn't just a repetition of sounds. It came out like a giant guttural whoop before almost every word. My fat crippled me as his stammer crippled him and there was, therefore, between us, a mutual sympathy.

I dominated. I asked the shopkeepers for things when we went to buy anything. I spoke for him when I could sense that it was difficult for him to speak for himself. Whenever he stammered my hand would go out to him, to hold his hand, to touch him, to offer him my sympathy, my love, my strength. Often he would practise saying 'caramel custard' six times in a row without stammering and I would praise him as a mother does her child.

His father approved of me immediately. My parents approved of him hesitantly. After the initial disappointment that he was not and did not intend to be either a doctor or a lawyer, they realized, with gratitude, that he was, at least, a Jew. He said he would return to the University the following year and study for an Arts Degree in Psychology part-time. This was almost acceptable. They did not approve of his stammer.

He was independent and self-willed. He belonged to himself in a way that I had never belonged to myself. He was clever enough to be anything, but cynical enough not to want to be anything. I admired that. He was not propelled towards the making of money, did not, in fact, care much about it at all. I liked that. He was socialistic in politics and non-materialistic. I liked that. He acted out a defiance of my parents' values that I could not act out for myself. He believed in truth, self-analysis, facing problems and talking things out. I approved of all of that. He had, at ten, been classed as a mathematical genius. There was about him this air of extraordinary and untapped human intelligence. I thought him to be the cleverest person I had ever met. Perhaps I was right. I passed my examinations by hard work; he breezed through. I looked up to him because I thought he was cleverer than I was. I could see his potential and I believed that I had fallen in love with it.

His need for me bordered on desperation. His mother had died of cancer when he was fourteen and his step-mother proved to be unsatisfactory as a substitute. He longed for a mother, a sister, a friend. I had to be all three. I didn't mind. I always felt that one day people would realize why I'd chosen this stammering boy as my mate. He longed for children and wanted me to be their mother. He called me Pud, not because I was fat, but out of affection. He called my cunt Mabel and I called his prick Frankie. I don't remember why.

I was in love with the idea of marriage. I believed I was in love with him. I longed to be engaged, to wear a diamond ring, to flaunt to my parents and to all the world the fact that a man wanted to marry me. He never proposed to me. We just assumed that we would marry. My sister had been planning her engagement but I needed to get in first and I did, to her despair, announce my engagement before her. I had to assert my rightful place as the older sister. We went to my uncle, the jeweller, to choose a ring. My future husband had sixty pounds to spend and, to my eternal shame, I allowed my parents, without my fiancé's knowledge, to put in an extra thirty pounds, so that my diamond would be bigger.

I remember the engagement party and my endless smile. Hundreds of my parents' friends milling in our flat bringing silver, linen, dinner sets, ashtrays, endless salt and pepper shakers, hand towels, ugly vases – a truly Jewish engagement party. My pride – I had a man and a man, moreover, who loved me for what I was. How superior we felt, he and I, that we, perceptive and intelligent as we were, were able to see beneath the false faces and shams of society – to see true beauty and truth and the meaning of life. How adult we seemed to ourselves and to each other – how childish, now, on looking back.

Engagement is, for both of us, a time of growth. We are in no hurry to get married. We like being engaged. We have sufficient freedom and no responsibilities. My parents start to love this boy I am to marry. Their relief that I will not be an old maid is enormous. It is no less great than my own. I have two maiden aunts, sisters of my mother. The limitations of spinsterhood are horrifying to me. I feel secure behind my diamond ring. It is my protection and my defence. He is secure, too, and we bathe in the warmth of the marriage that will one day be.

My mother and I both see him as a deprived child. He is not treated well at home. My mother takes him over. Soon she is doing all his washing and he comes to our place for dinner every night. Finally she tells him that as she is already doing his washing and feeding him he might as well move in. My sister is soon to be married, my brother is overseas – there's room for him to live with us.

So we dwell in this strange but rather peaceful household. We go on with our studies. We are fed, looked after, provided for by my parents. We are, both of us, for the first time, the happy children of benevolent parents. In this glow of parental warmth we both blossom. Even sex is permitted – not officially, but always possible. We study in my room together at night. We wait for my parents to go to sleep and then we can make love before he returns to his room to sleep for the night. It is a perfect arrangement. Indeed, who would ever bother to get married under such idyllic circumstances. We go away for holidays together. My father, seeing only what he wants to see, gives us money towards our illicit weekends. He even offers to make motel bookings for us. We refuse, knowing that he'll book single rooms. We buy wedding rings from Woolworths and pretend to be married.

I feel that I should enjoy these weekends away more than I do. I am happier with our arrangements at home, because here our lovemaking is restricted by outside circumstances. When we are away there are no restrictions and this doesn't suit me. I find it difficult to sleep in a double bed. I tell myself that it's just that I'm not used to it. One time, we go away and find we've been allocated a twin-bedded room. He is irate; I am delighted.

He wants to make love to me all the time and I don't want to make love to him all the time. We are both well aware of the fact that he loves me more than I love him and that he wants me more than I want him. We analyze the situation, talk about it, try to understand it, try to come to terms with it. He longs to suck my nipples but if he so much as touches them I shudder with distaste. We try to sort out the problem. It is always my sexual problems that we are trying to analyze because he doesn't have any. We decide that my abhorrence for breast sucking must arise from my early and premature weaning. He therefore approaches the matter with delicacy and patience. It is one year before I allow him to kiss my breast, another year before I can let him suck them. He is, indeed, a tolerant man. When we are away together I wake up in the mornings to find his penis burning a bruise in my thigh, but I don't like to make love in the mornings and, again, we try to understand why. I don't even want to make love every day and in the whole seventeen years I am to know him we never make love twice on one day.

I am aware, as he is, of my sexual inadequacies. I have periods of real frigidity and sometimes I go for weeks without an orgasm. He has become an expert lover now, calm, patient, slow, knowing every part of my body, trying to please and always, always waiting for me. He can wait, even if it takes two hours to make me come. We aim always at the perfection of a mutual orgasm. We see no value in coming alone. If I don't make it he is filled with a despair so great that I start to pretend to reach a climax. I become good at pretending, to please him.

We are, then, aware of my low libido, my lack of intense sexuality but we both believe that this is a problem we can face and overcome. I believe, at this stage, that I love him as much as it is possible for me to love. It is just that I am not capable of his quality of loving. We learn to live with it. I start each sexual encounter with him from the standpoint of resistance. He must gradually and slowly excite me, break down my barriers, make my orgasm inevitable. My climax is something he steals and wins from me, despite my resistance. It is not something that I give. I always feel that if he could just leave me alone for two or three days then I might come to him with my sexuality as a gift but he never gives me the time or space to want or need. He always takes; I never give – so it is to go on throughout our life together. I long for my periods because then I am allowed five days off. Sometimes, at the end of my period, I even want to make love but I never let on. Sex, right from the beginning, is a battleground, where he and I eternally act out a winner-loser theme. I feel guilty about my lack of sexuality and he knows this and plays with it. By the end of the first year of our engagement it is quite obvious that the only problems about our relationship are my problems. He has none.

We adopt a policy of total honesty with each other. We cannot lie. We know everything about each other – our inner-most thoughts, fantasies, hopes and dreams. We become each other – mould and blend, share and give, analyze and probe. We do not allow ourselves any bushes to hide behind but bravely face our inner truth, holding hands for mutual support in this relentless journey towards understanding ourselves and each other. He tries to help me with my eating and I try to help him with his stammer and all this probing and soul searching does get us somewhere. We do, indeed, start to grow up.

He is now working as an Employment Officer in a large company. His job is demanding and exhausting and involves a great deal of talking, interviewing, telephoning. He is determined to defeat his stammer. His employers don't even know that he has one. The effort makes him very tense and when he is with me he needs to unwind for hours, barely able to get a sentence out without faltering. But I, compassionate, loving, caring, take in, listen, discuss, analyze. We work together on everything.

I, meanwhile, am achieving. My ring protects me. Because it is there on my finger I feel smug and secure. I can meet and talk to people, even to other men, because I am engaged and therefore safe. I blossom intellectually. I find that I'm good at English and do so well that I'm doing distinction work and hope to go on to an Honours degree. I start to write, hesitantly at first. A few poems make their way into a university magazine and then I write a short play. I go on to write a full length play and I am astounded by the fact that I share first prize in a university play writing competition. I win a typewriter. I really know where I am going. I see the man I am going to marry as the secure and loving background from which I can venture out to face the world. I would like to be more unconventional than I am but I am not really revolutionary at all. Jewish girls are supposed to remain virgins until they marry and this is the only area in which I rebel. I admire rebellion in others, though, and I would like to be part of it. I go along to a meeting of those who believe in free love because I feel there should be some bonds of similarity between me and the members of this group. Germaine Greer, as yet unknown, is addressing the meeting. She uses the word 'fuck' and I'm so shocked that I leave the meeting in horror.

I think I'm being educated but education really passes me by. I study philosophy under Professors Anderson and Stout but I have no idea what either of them is talking about. I study government but don't understand the first thing about Marxism. I study anthropology but never grasp the social implications of the subject. I study history but never once break through the insulated shell of my bourgeois Jewish upbringing. Only in literature do I shine for here the world of words is a galaxy of imaginary lives. I love the game of delving for meaning, the deep analysis of texts. This is my talent and I lose myself in it. For four years I am allowed to read and read, and write a little. A wonderful time, looking back.

An older student was in my first-year English class. I noticed him but never spoke to him. The next year he went on to do distinction work in psychology. I met him that year through a mutual friend. Strange man he was – so neat and tidy, white faced and balding head, black tie and shiny shoes, ice-blue eyes.

I am sitting with him now in a curved stone archway in the University quadrangle on a late summer, bird-gathering afternoon. He is talking to me and I am talking to him and I don't understand him because he is all that I am not. I've noticed that he's often alone and that he seems to frighten people away. He has the psychology student's deplorable habit of analyzing others and I imagine that it is for this reason that other students avoid him. He tries to do the same thing with me but I am so involved in analyzing myself that nothing he says to me can upset me. This failure to disturb me seems to break down some barrier for him and he starts to really communicate with me. We become friends.

He starts to tell me about himself, hesitantly at first. Because I don't laugh at him, he gives more and because I don't discourage him, he feels comfortable with me. I learn a very strange mixture of facts – that his mother is large, Italian and dark; that he has a small step-brother whom he hates; that he used to play the trombone in a pop band; that he polishes his shoes every day; that he experiences revelations; that he can never afford to eat lunch; that his father, who died when he was six, was God; that he longs to be Jewish because he feels persecuted and if only he were Jewish there would be some rationale for his persecution; that he is embarrassed by the fact that he is going bald; that he has developed and written down a world theory that explains satisfactorily the nature of existence; that he can only love Jewish women; that he will be world famous by the time he is thirty.

I believe it all and I'm very impressed because I've never known anyone like him before and we have between us a rare and beautiful thing – a perfect platonic relationship. But then he does something to disturb me because he presents to me the idea that no relationship can be purely platonic and he tells me that he believes that there is, flowing beneath our friendship, a current of unexpressed sexuality. What he is saying shocks me but as his hand moves toward mine I can almost anticipate what will happen and his touch ignites something between us and a flood response is released in me and my smugness is shattered, my security destroyed. He and I now spend our days in secret kissing, hugging, touching, wanting. We sit in the library and write smouldering, passionate poems to each other.

I don't know what to do. I cannot tell the man I am to marry and I carry my guilt about with me. It is not so much guilt for what I'm doing but guilt for not telling him what I'm doing. I realize, from the way that I want this man, that perhaps I've never know real wanting before. My desire throws in doubt the whole concept of my sexual inadequacies. I float, like a helpless victim, in the stream of my passion and I know I must act it out.

It is not so easy to find a place to go because he lives in a boarding house and it seems impossible to use my home. Perhaps we are both afraid. We just go on wanting, touching, kissing, but not consummating our love. Perhaps we really want to keep it that way. But I am determined to have him and I tell some lies and get my parents' car one night and we go down to Coogee Beach. We've been waiting for this moment for months and as we tear off our clothes I clutch at him, ready to come at a touch. But it's no good, no good at all. He can't get his penis erect. I don't know what to do and all I can feel is fury and frustration. I shout. I scream. I cry. I pull on my clothes. I jerk the car to a start. I drive stormily home. I never want to see him again.

But I see him again the next day and he tries to explain his impotence away in terms of over-excitement. He is quite sure that the next time he'll be alright. We arrange a next time but the same thing happens and we part in dumb disbelief.

Then he writes me a letter. He says that he cannot make love to me because I am engaged to marry someone else. He says that he loves me and asks me to make a choice. I feel that he is forcing me to face something that I do not want to face. He is asking me to look at myself but I don't look very hard. I do not even hesitate in deciding to remain with the Jewish boy and I even pretend to myself that this experience has made me realize just how much I love the man I am to marry. I am like a rabbit scurrying back to the dark, enclosed, security of its burrow. It will be a long, long time before I ever dare to look at another man with love.

A year later the man whose love I have rejected takes his own life on the sand dunes at Cronulla. I am overwhelmed then with the burden of my guilt and I must confess my sexual misdemeanours to my mate, letting every detail spill out of me, longing to be forgiven, needing the absolution that only he can give. And he, tolerant, kind, understanding forgives me – or so it seems.

I dwell now in the smug security of doing the right thing. I am fulfilling all my obligations. My parents are proud of my university results and proud of the boy I will marry. As he climbs higher in the business world they become more and more satisfied with my choice. Time and my support and the enormous effort he exerts himself have given him assurance and self-confidence. To everyone's relief the horrible stammer is largely under control.

I swim in his love which is, apparently, endless, sincere, devoted. I cannot believe that anyone has ever been loved as much as he loves me. We both still agree that, essentially, I am the kind of person who cannot love as deeply, as devotedly as he can so I still look up to him, as a creature of greater emotional capacity. Sometimes I think of the man who killed himself. Often I think I see him coming towards me as I walk down the street. I go to touch him and he disappears. He haunts the shadows of my dreams. He is the road I did not take and I carry him like a burden beneath my breast.

I go on writing but I do not dare to tell anyone what fantasies I have about my plays. I imagine myself on stage, being wildly applauded by the audience as my powerful play proves to be an overnight success. And when I write I don't need to eat. It is as if all the frustration, hatred, anger and despair that goes into the tearing apart and swallowing of food can be projected into my characters. I create instead of destroying. My writing keeps me sane.

I write a play about my family. It is a very melodramatic play but it has moments of real power. I call it The Angry Child and I make myself the central character. In my play I am the scapegoat of everyone else's emotions, the Cinderella drudge. And then I meet a man who helps me find myself. He discovers in me a wish to write a novel but he cannot get me to write for my own sake so he pretends to be in love with me and he locks me up and makes me write until my magical best-seller is complete. I triumph, tell all the family to go to hell as if I'm going to make it as a human being after all. The man thinks I'm strong enough to carry on without him but he's wrong and when he tells me he doesn't love me I kill him and kill myself.

And my play is the truth, really, for I cannot live without love. I, who had such a short encounter with the soft breast, need always to be cradled and held. And that is what the man I am to marry offers me. He cannot stop touching me, always longs to hold me and it is that kind of fusion that I need. So the man becomes the thing I have lacked and longed for. He becomes a mother to me. And I become a mother to him, for he longs, as I do, for the good mother touch. So we each become to the other the good breast, the soft warmth, the eternal flow of giving.

By the end of my last year at university we have been engaged for four years. It is time to marry. It cannot reasonably be postponed any longer. I know, deep down in myself, in a place where I will not look, that what I feel for this man is not what a woman is supposed to feel when she marries. I know, somewhere, in the very bones of my being, that I am a writer and that I should break all ties with my family and with the man who so desperately wants to marry me. I see what I am and I see what I could be and I turn my back on this vision of self and I marry him instead.

I like to tell myself now that I was the helpless victim of my upbringing, my environment, my conditioning and my middle class Jewish values, that there was no choice for me but marriage. But that would be a lie. There was a choice and the truth of the matter is that I married him out of a terrible and desperate need to be loved.

The marriage ceremony and the celebration afterwards elate me. I am tiny. I weigh seven stone. I wear a short dress of guipure lace and I am beautiful. It is my day. I can't stop smiling and I know that I am going to live happily ever after. I'm not at all depressed on my wedding night and feel even better when I have an orgasm and he doesn't. Such a thing has never happened to him before. Perhaps marriage bothers him more than he'd care to admit. It obviously doesn't bother me at all. I'm doing just fine.

We don't have much money for a honeymoon so we've just booked in to a motel at Nowra, a hundred miles down the on the south coast. It's raining as we leave Sydney but I don't mind. I'm married and I'm off to start a new life. It's the 22nd of December, 1961.

We arrive at the motel and he wants to make love as soon as we get there. I don't want to but he didn't come last night and he's randy and that's not fair and what's a honeymoon for anyway. All I want is for it to be over quickly but he goes on and on, grinding into me. It's so distasteful to me that I can't even pretend I'm enjoying it. I lie there like a lifeless fish. I feel guilty. How appalling it must be to make love to a woman who doesn't respond. I wriggle around a bit but my heart's not in it and I feel repelled by his sexuality. He is determined to win.

He goes on and on but I can't come. He concedes defeat and as he comes I can feel his bitterness pouring into me.

We go out to have lunch. I tell him I want to eat fish and chips. That's the most fattening thing I can think of. We eat fish and chips. Then I want a milkshake and a chocolate and an ice cream. I watch him watching me eat. 'I can't help it,' I say, 'I have to eat.'

'Every time you can't cope sexually, you stuff yourself with food,' he says. I go on eating. I can't deny what he's said because it's true. He has placed me in an intolerable position. I am, on the whole, a secret and private eater. I don't like anyone else seeing what I do to myself. Now I'm trapped because I have to eat and I can't go anywhere to do it. I can't give way completely to my need to go on stuffing myself with food. I can neither express nor escape it.

There's nothing to do. It's still raining. We read books for a while but my eyes can't take in the words. All I can think of is cream cakes and bread and honey and ice cream with hot chocolate sauce. I've got to escape but there's no escape. I've no excuse to go anywhere. Before long he's cuddling up to me, gentle, soft, sorry for being angry with me, cajoling, touching, wanting. Now I really want to scream. All I want is food and he's offering me a prick, hard and hot. I make excuses. I tell him I won't be able to come and he'll be upset about that and it will all be screwed up again. He gives up trying.

In a way I want him to be angry with me. I would like him to shout at me, scream at me, storm out of the motel. If he did that I'd be able to rush to the nearest shop and gobble up chocolate and lollies. But he never reacts the way I want him to – always calm, always reasonable, always logical. He decides, instead, that we should talk it out, analyze our sexual failures of the last twenty-four hours. We talk, or rather, he talks until it's all sorted out to our satisfaction. We are both more affected by the actual step of marriage than we thought we would be. We just have to get used to our new state. We don't really like being stuck here in a motel in the rain even though that might be someone else's idea of a perfect honeymoon. We have a flat in Sydney that we are ready to move into so let's call the honeymoon a failure and return to our own home the next morning. I am deeply relieved at this decision, feeling once again how lucky I am to have married a man who has such tolerance of my seemingly endless inadequacies. Before we go to sleep I let him squeeze all the pimples and blackheads he can find on my face and behind my ears and on my back. I really don't have many but he searches for them like a mother monkey de-fleaing her child. Such activity calms him. I feel purified by his removal of any scrap of offensive dirt from the pores of my skin. I wish he could as effectively cleanse my soul.

The flat is an old one in an old suburb. One bedroom, an old bathroom, a fridge that rattles through the night, musty old furniture. When you are just married it should not matter where you are for you are alone together and free. It matters to us. We are depressed and we blame our depression on our dingy surroundings. I am guiltily aware that our depression is entirely due to me. I cannot stop eating and I start to get fat again and when I over-eat I can't make love partly because my stomach is so full that if he lies on top of me I want to spew and partly because the very fact that I'm over-eating indicates that I'm not coping with life.

I can tell myself that it's because I'm teaching for the first time. I've never taught before and I've been given this job as Senior English Mistress at a private girls' school. I keep swallowing appetite control pills in some desperate hope that they will curb my eating but I've been taking them for so many years that they have little or no effect. On the other hand, I'm terrified that if I stop taking them I'll eat up the world. I suppose I'm addicted to them but I don't like to think about that.

The most significant thing about the school I'm teaching at is that fresh, iced, buttered buns are offered free to the staff at morning tea time and fresh, iced cakes are offered for afternoon tea. Each morning's lessons become the background; in the foreground is the struggle of will I or won't I have any buttered bun for morning tea. I always decide, quite sensibly, that I won't. Then we sit down, all female staff, of course, to morning tea. I watch everyone else eating. The next step is to say, 'It's not fair, why shouldn't I have some,' then my hand takes a piece and my mouth swallows it. I even tell myself that just because I have one piece of buttered bun it need not mean that I have to stuff myself with food all day. I trick myself each time. One mouthful and I am lost. I marvel at other people's ability to eat a piece of buttered bun and then walk off as if nothing serious has happened.

I come home at night and confess to him, list my eating misdemeanours as I did to my mother in the bath. The resolution is the same as it was with her. He absolves me and I determine to be good tomorrow. He never comments on the fact that I'm getting fatter. He loves me whatever size I am, so if he doesn't care, then why do I? But I do care. In fact it's the only thing I care about at all, the focus of my existence, the centre of my waking thoughts. It is surprising that, with such a history of failure, I should wake up each morning with belief in success.

The thing that disturbs me most about being married is that I have to share a bed. Within a few weeks of my marriage I realize that I have a very real problem. I can't listen to the man, my husband, sleeping beside me. I lie there and I know that I have to go to sleep before him. If I go to sleep before he does then I won't have to listen to him breathe while he is asleep. Because I'm trying so hard to go to sleep before he does, I can't go to sleep at all. So mostly he goes to sleep before me and I lie there waiting for it to happen. I pretend I can't hear the deep, regular breaths. I try to think of other things. Then I am aware that I am consciously thinking of other things so that I won't have to listen to him breathing. His face is turned towards me and one arm reaches out in sleep to hold and touch me. If he faces me then I not only hear but also feel the soft regularity of his breath. I lie there trying not to let it happen and trying to be calm. I try to adjust my breathing pattern to his in the hope that my pattern will then be able to obliterate his. I try but it's his pattern that I imitate and because it's his and not mine it doesn't feel natural to me. It's not possible for me to go to sleep while I'm breathing with his rhythm. I can feel the anxiety begin to tingle in my forehead, find a scream rising in my throat. I fight it down. This is my beloved husband sleeping peacefully by my side. It's no good. I want to scream. Each breath is an intrusion, biting, slicing into me. Each breath cuts into my brain, crowds me, devours me. I have no space, no air. The scream fills my throat. I bounce noisily in the bed to relieve my tension. He stirs. I hope he'll wake up. I am about to panic. I nudge him, make him roll over. He mumbles but doesn't wake. If I can make him lie with his head turned the other way then perhaps my anxiety will subside. The momentary improvement makes me feel almost peaceful. I start to drift in my own fantasies, lulled and calm. Suddenly I hear him again. He's bloody well breathing! And what can I do now? He's already turned the other way. I have a series of devices to try. Firstly I use cotton wool and stuff up my ears so that I can't hear him. For ten minutes this works but then his breathing eats through the cotton wool and I am trapped again by his regular, rhythmic breath. I pretend I'm asleep and 'accidentally' kick him, viciously. He half wakes, mumbles, breathes less loudly for a short while. Then it settles back into regularity again, deeper, deeper. The deeper he breathes the more disturbed I become. I want to bite and scream and bash my head in. No, I don't want to bash my head in; I want bash his head in, smash him and crush him and kill him. I don't know why. That's what's so frightening.

It is early in our marriage and I still hope that I will overcome this problem. Finally I shake him away crying, 'I can't sleep! You snore!' he awakes, apologetic, and I feel guilty because he doesn't snore at all. Why do I behave in this peculiar way? I don't know the answer and neither does he so he approaches the whole matter in a reasonable and logical way. He now reads a book or the newspaper while I am going to sleep and he doesn't go to sleep himself until he is quite sure that I am asleep. The vision of this husband as the man of perfect understanding grows and grows. I am grateful to him for putting up with me. His approach to the problem sometimes works, but if I wake with a start in the night then the whole terrible thing begins again.

After a while I find a new solution. I buy earplugs. He hates me wearing them because he feels that I'm shutting him out, rejecting him. He's right. So I hide the earplugs under my pillow and when I think he's not noticing I put them in. If he thinks I've worn them, then he sulks in the morning so I try to pretend that I haven't used them at all. Sometimes one of the earplugs escapes from under my pillow and I wake in the middle of the night in a state of panic. I cannot survive without them now. For a long time I try to deal with this problem. It is a nightly terror to me. I battle with my eating every day, with my sexuality (or lack of it) every second night and with his breathing every night. I am, decidedly, not normal. I know that. My abnormalities serve to bind me further and further into an attitude of sincere gratitude towards him for his constant love and understanding.

What I long for, really, is a space about myself. Sleeping is, for me, a very personal thing. I like to drift to sleep on my own thoughts and wake again to a sense of my own being. Anyone sleeping beside me intrudes into my being to an intolerable degree.

I come back now to the small London bedroom. I turn and look at the man from Ceylon sleeping beside me. He repulses me. I feel that I hate him and all the men who have ever expected me to sleep beside them. I kick the covers off. My throat feels dry. My hand goes down to touch my clitoris, gently at first, then more and more swiftly. It feels good. Suddenly my hand becomes a penis and I move and touch and weave and thrust, gently, then firmly to suit myself and I build and climb and soar and fly bringing myself to a shattering climax, crying and coming and wetting and flooding all over his nice white sheets.

I look at the clock. 5 am. The tube will be running. With a sense of elation I quietly pull on my clothes. I don't want to wake him because I don't want to talk to him. I want to pretend he doesn't exist.

I walk down two flights of stairs and out into the cold London air. I want to shout and laugh and dance and skip and jump and run. My joy is wild, beyond belief. For I am free! Not because I have escaped from the brown man in the oppressive room but because I have escaped from all men. I never need to have a man make love to me again because this morning I have achieved something I have never done before. I have masturbated to orgasm for the first time in my whole life. I have, at last, been able to perform a gesture of self love.

SIX

I go back to my hotel and slip into the luxury of my large London bathtub. I look at my body with new appreciation as it half floats in the white tub. I wash away the brown man's sperm and wonder, idly, why I've been relying on men for all these years when I could have been relying on myself.

It is 6.30 am. Too early to start the day. My room is comfortably warm and I get into bed and stretch naked in the fresh white sheets. I feel calm now. My hands run gently down my body, feeling the outlines of its shape, its form. I have always floated in my own confusion, unable to feel the outline of my extremities, not knowing where my body ends and the air begins, spilling into the atmosphere. I have always relied on my collision with others to provide me with a mirror for my own image. But now I have found my own curve, entered my own skin – snug, secure, sweetly self-contained. And as I lie there, quiet and still, my soft breath flows from I to me and I am one, integrated, complete, and I barely dare to move in the hushed and precious moment of my knowing.

And there was the glimmer of a similar feeling once, just once in the marriage long ago. There was a swift moment when I almost believed that I held myself, my fate and my future, curled there in the palm of my hand.

It is the second year of the marriage and the second year of teaching and we have moved to a new, bright, modern flat and it seems to me that life is a little easier to handle. He is preoccupied with work and the fact that he is working so hard gives me a little space around myself. When I come home from school in the afternoon I have hours alone. I curl up in the big lounge chair and think. He has taken away my precious thinking time before I go to sleep and when I wake up in the morning but now I can think in the afternoon instead. I have to get up out of the chair to cook his dinner. I wish I could sit there forever.

While I am sitting in the chair each afternoon, something is happening inside my head. There is a pressure in my brain. There is a play inside me. I do not yet know what the play will be. All I know is that it is filling me up. I let it build and grow. Soon my fingers start to itch to hold a pen, my hand impatient to play its role. I have a typewriter but I cannot create that way. I must feel the pen, touch the paper, have the flow from head to hand to pen to paper. And when it comes my writing is unconscious, dictated by my inner self, compulsively thrust from my entrails, spilled onto the page.

Finally the play explodes and I become the vehicle for its birth. I sit there for three days and three nights. I do not sleep. I barely eat. I am totally uncaring of anything or anyone around me. All I do is write. And he is, of course, kind and understanding, tolerant and undemanding. He is, on the surface, delighted by the fact that I am writing again.

God is the central character in my play. I have been reading the Old Testament and the early concept of God intrigues me. He seems to be an aggressive, authoritarian, tyrannical old man. My play is called The Creator and it becomes a retelling of the Garden of Eden story with God presented as a ridiculous and petty old fool. God's companion in heaven is the angel, Gabriel, but my Gabriel is a Cockney-accented, humorous, rough and ready servant to God's will. There is no serpent in my Garden; Man decides to leave the Garden of his own free will.

I am delighted as the play takes on its own form, writing itself forward. The thing that pleases me most is that I'm not in it. I don't seem to be involved. Then I realize, with a sense of shock, that I am God. I have been deluding myself. I have wanted to believe that I, the creator, am outside the things I create. But I am God and I am Man and I am Woman and I am the stupid angel Gabriel; I am and must be all my characters. Their only existence is the life I give them, their only actions those I control, their only words those I write. I know then that the play is about creating. I am using God's creation of the world as the symbol through which I am examining the role each person plays in the creating and moulding of his or her own life. I, who have been almost entirely fashioned by others, am writing a play full of the confidence in Man's ability to make his own decisions to direct his own life. I do not see this irony.

I finish my play, exhausted but fulfilled. And then I do what I always do with anything I write – I give it to him to evaluate.

He insists that he criticises my work objectively and I believe that to be true. His criticism is usually of the kind that points to jarring words, outworn clichés or failure to sustain characterization. He has an intense interest in the origin and meaning of words, a very wide vocabulary and a precise power and control over words that I believe to be superior to my own. So, during these sessions, although I feel like shouting, screaming and stamping my feet, I sit there quietly, accepting unquestioningly that he is right. And he is right – always. I can tell that he is right because he has a logical, well-supported reason for every criticism he makes. I see myself as illogical, unreasonable, emotional. I need his clear, cool head to correct, contain, control my writing. He enjoys criticising my work. He enjoys it partly because it is an intellectual exercise in which he can show his superior perceptive and logical ability; partly because it is his way of breaking back into my consciousness because I have rejected him while I have been writing and he can now, vicariously, become a part of my creative processes; partly because he is jealous and would like to write himself and, therefore, enjoys this partial destruction of the thing I've so carefully and painfully built up; partly because, in our relationship, he must always be the parent teaching the correct way to the somewhat chaotic and undisciplined child.

So I sit there, tense, waiting for the verdict. And the verdict does matter. I can't pretend it doesn't. It is his seal of approval that I need. I cannot function without it. I'm expecting the picking at individual words but I don't get it. This time I get something different. He looks at me. 'It's a terrific play,' he says, 'but you'll have to rewrite the whole of the third act.' I can't move. He goes on. I've been sloppy and sentimental, haven't understood my theme properly, haven't executed it truly. I see what he means. He is, as usual, right.

I rewrite immediately and within a day produce a new third act. 'That's more like it,' he says. Now we start the bit by bit, word by word, nit-picking. I want to scream. My play is a child and he is citicising the shape of its toes, the colour of its hair, the texture of its skin. I listen, absorb, accept.

I begin a total rewrite and another and another. Never has he been so relentless, never have I worked so hard to get a play into shape. Finally, it is finished and I know that I have written something good enough for production. I type it out, give it to people to read, send it to producers. It is a time before nudity is permitted on stage and my play calls for Man and Woman to act in the nude. Potential producers express doubts as to how they could overcome this problem. But the important thing is the knowledge that the play is good and, for the moment, that is all that matters. The frustrations involved in getting something produced on stage do not concern me yet. I am happy to bask in the praise that people shower on me.

A surprising thing about the play is that it is actually funny. It is not primarily a comedy but it has a lot of humour in both dialogue and situation. My husband is always telling me that I have no sense of humour and no sense of fun. He's right, of course. I can never remember jokes and have no talent for the sharp, witty retorts that he is so readily able to supply. So now I feel, for a short while, a sense of belief in myself. I equate myself with Man in my play. Like him, I have accepted the responsibility for what I am and what I will be. I believe that, in the very act of writing the play, I have taken over the controlling and the shaping of my own destiny. But I am tricked. I have created what is to become a final and terrible irony of self-deception. For it is the male Jewish God that I have examined, the God to whom Jewish men pray each day, saying:

> *Blessed art thou, O Lord our God, King of the Universe, who has not made me a woman.'*

To whom the Jewish women reply:

> *Blessed art thou, O Lord our God, King of the Universe, who has made me according to Thy will.'*

I have unmasked God the Father but I have not found the benign face of the Mother God within. The Greeks of the ancient world found her in their goddess Athena – all-protecting, all-giving, all-powerful. But she is as remote to me as that long-dead world. The creative force of Woman eludes me still.

And now that I have committed my act of aggression, taken my pen and written my play, forced it out of me and carved it down with the thrust of my male sword, exposed it to his scalpel for its final dissection and refinement – now I am so empty that my inner caverns ache and reverberate their hollowness. He knows the time is right. He wants to inhabit my echoing spaces, thrust his penis into my darkness, spill his sperm into my womb and fill me up with a child.

I am so depleted that I dream of being emptied out. It is a dream of spring cleaning. He is emptying my house so that he can clean it up and get it all into order. I am so weak that I cannot help him. I lie there in my bed watching him carry out all my furniture. I long to keep all my mess about me but he won't let me and I do not have the strength to stop him. Relentlessly, he empties my room and puts all my precious possessions down on the beach while he cleans out my empty room. Suddenly I am on the beach and I am naked. He has even stripped me of my clothes and I watch helplessly as an enormous wave comes and swallows up all the things that are me. He comes up to me. I scream at him. 'Look what you've done.' I beat him with my fists. 'I'm sorry,' he says, 'I only meant to sort everything out for you.' I watch my manuscripts, plays and poems and stories, watch them swept away and destroyed by the sea.

The play I have written is the last shout, the final scream. Now I give in, the willing victim, the empty shell, the eternal slave – longing to be whipped, to be punished, to be destroyed. I am not a man with a penis, a pen or a sword and I must accept whatever retribution is in store for me. I have tried to fight with a man's weapons and now I am the wounded soldier, withdrawn from battle – the castrated eunuch. I am a shadowy reflection of an imagined self. I agree to have a baby.

He's always wanted babies. Why does he want them so desperately? Why does he want them more than I do? Why is his paternal instinct more developed than my maternal one? I put it down to the fact that I'm always inadequate in emotional responses and see this phenomenon as further proof of his emotional superiority. He is impatient to become a father. He would like to have six children – I have serious doubts about having just one. However, I know I can rely on him. He will know how to look after our children, even if I don't. I feel a total confidence in him. I cannot imagine being afraid of death, if I should die in his arms.

We become natural childbirth fanatics and indulge in endless discussions on how important it is for him to be present at the birth, how we will breast feed, toilet train, discipline and educate our children. We are obsessed. Everything is talked about, agreed upon, sorted out.

The only problem is that I can't seem to get pregnant. In our naivety we think it will happen straight away but it doesn't. We are so sure that I will conceive immediately that I give up work in preparation for the great event. This gives me all day and every day to worry about the fact that I'm not getting pregnant.

We decide, when I leave work, to move in with my parents for a while so that we can save enough money to buy or build a house. This seems reasonable to everyone. My brother and sister are both married and my parents live in a very large and beautiful flat at Darling Point. As both my parents and my husband go to work, I am the only one not working. My mother has someone to clean the flat. All I have to do is a bit of ironing and help to get dinner at night. My job is clearly defined – it is my responsibility to get pregnant.

And I see it totally in these terms. There cannot be anything wrong with him. He is a vigorous, sexual, normal young man. The fault must lie with me. After three months I'm sure I'm sterile. My ability to orgasm is constantly in jeopardy as anxiety causes almost total frigidity. This leads to further guilt. Am I sterile because I'm not having orgasms? Even if this is not true I think it is true and I get more and more anxious.

Living with my parents is causing tension as well. For me, this anxiety starts at dinner time. My mother cracks her jaws down on her food and gulps it down half-chewed. I can't stand to listen to her eat. It's as if she's devouring chunks of me with every mouthful. That's when the scream starts welling up inside me, almost bursting out of my throat. I have to keep it down. At the moment when I know I can't stand it any longer she suddenly finishes, jumps up from the table and is ready to wash up the dishes before the rest of us are even half-way through our dinner.

My father has developed a kind of nervous habit about eating. In the middle of a mouthful, his mouth suddenly becomes paralysed and he can't go on and he sits for five or six seconds – frozen, statue-like – before he can continue eating. Every time he does it I panic. It fills me with terror because I think he's going to die. What is it that makes him gag like that? Do they both eat people? Suddenly, it's as if I'm being devoured by mother and father, one on each side of me, tearing off my flesh. I want to rush from the table, escape from their jaws but I have to sit there and endure it. It is obvious to me that my reactions are unusual. Perhaps I am even abnormal. But how can I be sure? I feel they are biting me and chewing me and swallowing me.

My father's nervous sniff and nervous cough also bother me. Very often the four of us play cards after dinner. The tension mounts in me and every sniff or cough is like a knife slicing into me. Again I have to suppress a scream. I want to throw down the cards and hurl over the table and smash and shatter and kill. But I can't do that so I just sit there, playing cards, as if I'm a perfectly normal human being. No one even suspects the murderous rage that I keep caged inside me. By the time the evening is over I feel as if I am in shreds but the night is not over for me yet; I still have to face the attempt at baby-making followed by the intrusive breathing of the man sleeping beside me.

I read a lot of books to fill in the time but I am very bored and very unhappy. Even someone who had never been a compulsive eater might well become one under these circumstances. I certainly resort to the only thing left that gives me comfort. I stuff myself with food. I have been slim for two years, the longest success I've ever had and now I stand helplessly by and watch while a part of me eats and eats and covers up my little self with ugly rolls of fat. I am powerless to stop its progress – a minute speck in the ocean of my instincts.

After four months I go to a gynaecologist. He says he won't look at me until my husband has a sperm count. I am astounded. He is shocked too, but we have to obey the rules. We have to have intercourse and then, instead of coming inside me, he has to withdraw and come in the jar. Not only does he have to do this, but he has to do it in the morning so that I can take the sperm straight into town for analysis. It's a ludicrous business. If I were someone else I might be able to laugh about it but it's gross and monstrous to me and I can't see it as funny. It even bothers him. He can't ejaculate the first time; the second morning he succeeds. I sense in him a momentary anxiety in having his manhood actually put to the test but he passes with flying colours and the fault is very swiftly returned to its rightful place – with me. Now I have to keep a temperature graph to determine my time of ovulation. I can't just get up in the morning, like everyone else, and go to the toilet. I have to lie there for three minutes with a thermometer up my vagina and check and record the results.

At least this cuts down on the number of our sexual encounters. I can study the graph, tell him when the time of ovulation has arrived, have intercourse frantically for three days and then forget about it for a while. It's very nerve-wracking and our love making lacks any kind of spontaneity or real feeling. It has become a business enterprise.

It's now August and it's my birthday. I am twenty-six years old. I feel very fat. My slacks are two-way stretch and I'm putting the stretch to its absolute limit. It's very cold. I'm wearing a jumper and a big loose cardigan to hide the bulges at my hips and thighs. He's decided to take the day off from work and take me on an outing to the Blue Mountains for the day. I feel ugly. I never want to go anywhere when I feel ugly. I feel old and I feel depressed. He's depressed too, though he tries not to be because it's my birthday. We drive to Katoomba.

We are sitting eating lunch in the Paragon Café. They have marvellous home-made chocolates and all I can think about is whether I will dare to ask him to buy me some.

Suddenly he looks at me. 'Why can't you wear a bit of lipstick,' he says, 'when you go out with me? And couldn't you have brushed your hair before you got out of the car?' I am shocked. He has never said anything like this to me before. No matter how ugly or fat I have thought myself to be, he has never found me ugly. In fact, he has always laughed at me, said jokingly, his stiff penis digging into my thigh, 'You're so fat and ugly I can't bear to make love to you.' Any remnant of self esteem I might have had left now slides away from me. I am sexually inadequate, unable to conceive, and ugly. I feel his distaste gnawing into me. I don't dare to ask for any chocolates.

Now I am not just depressed and unhappy; I am desperate. My desperation makes no sense so I cannot talk of it to anyone. Some couples take years to conceive and we've only been trying for six months. But I feel useless and sterile and can see nothing but a blank vision of the appalling emptiness of a childless woman.

Fortunately, I contract flu and bronchitis and I am able to go to bed for two weeks without anyone considering it a strange thing to do. I would very much like to die but, of course, I'm much too healthy for that to happen. A terrible illness would do. I have the fantasy of contracting polio or meningitis – of lying in hospital for weeks at death's door, of my husband sitting beside me and talking me back to life with love and care and attention, of waking up, six weeks later, to find myself well, alive and at least two stone lighter. So much for fantasy. Although ill, I'm not as ill as I pretend to be and definitely not too ill to eat. I'm never too ill to eat. I think he feels guilty. During the second week of my illness he comes home with a present. It is a beautiful watch with a diamond on each side and a soft, black, velvet band. He says it is the gift he had intended to give me when I became pregnant but thinks I might need it now. I cry tears of gratitude. This dear, wonderful husband, so finely tuned to me, so keen in his insight, so realizing that I'm nearly destroyed brings me a gift of love, lifts me back to life.

My brother and his wife burst into the room. I want to show them my beautiful new watch but they don't give me a chance. They are bursting with excitement. They are pregnant and they weren't even trying. She was using a diaphragm. It was mistake but isn't it all delightful. How can they be so cruel?

When they leave he holds me and I cry like a child. What is my watch compared with their baby? What's wrong with me? My sister has two children, both mistakes. My brother's wife is pregnant, by mistake. Am I the only sterile one? He calms me, soothes me, caresses me, loves me, pulls me out of my despair.

Two months later the doctor tells me that I'm pregnant. I want to feel happy but the primary feeling is that of relief. I've made it. I even send a silent prayer of thanks to God, just in case he exists. And now my husband, my father and my mother express their joy. I become a worthy object in all their eyes. I have some value, after all. I am capable of being the receptacle for the foetal nurturing of a child. Amen.

I take to pregnancy as if it were the thing I was created for. There is purpose in my existence, meaning in my life. A child lives and grows within me and I am filled with the wonder of it. I go on a strict, healthy diet immediately and I stick to it so well that at the end of my pregnancy I weigh only three pounds more than I did at the beginning – an incredible feat. Who cares about plays and writing now! I am the Creator. I am bringing forth life. I love my body now, watch my nipples change colour, smooth and massage them each day so that they will be ready to give milk to my child. I fondle the soft curves of my belly, stroke the swelling mound. I love myself and he loves me. He doesn't just love me; he worships me. My body is his temple now, my womb his icon. He bows his head before me.

I am the Queen. I have never been the Queen before. My father, my mother, my husband all bend before me. I am the centre of the world, the axis of the universe. No reality exists but the life that is growing inside me. I am turned entirely, irrevocably within. I know what it is to laugh, to smile, to be happy.

And when the time comes he is with me on that longest of days. He knows what I must do as well as I know it myself and he is beside me constantly – encouraging, soothing, helping. We work and sweat together. Yet the final moment is mine alone for the moment of birth brings me a knowledge that only a woman can possess. And as I hold my son, wet and bloody in my hands, I feel, in that instant, the mighty fusion of life and death. I am a woman at last – eternal, fertile, flowing. Life, death; womb, tomb. I know and understand it all.

I understand the experience I have undergone. What I do not understand is the product of that experience. I examine him minutely and I find that I do not comprehend him at all. He does not in any way fulfil my expectations of what my child should look like. He has short, straight, fair hair and we both have curly, brown hair. He has grey eyes and we both have dark, brown eyes. His eyes are like a cat's, almond shaped. No one in the family has eyes like that. He is totally alien, yet totally mine. And how could I, out of my female self, have produced a male child? It seems both miraculous and frightening.

I do not really understand this little child and I do not really know how to be a mother. I have plenty of milk and I know how to feed him. That's the only thing I'm good at. I expect that after I've fed him he'll go to sleep but he doesn't seem to understand about sleep. He just cries. My husband insists that if the child cries then he needs attention. He must be either fed or picked up and cuddled and held whenever he cries. After one week I'm so exhausted that I beg my husband to let me get a nurse for a week so that she can teach me what to do. He refuses. There's no doubt in his mind that he can solve the problem.

During the day the child is my responsibility. I bathe him, feed him endlessly, walk him, cuddle him. He is like a little koala bear, snuggling into my neck, perfectly happy as long as he is constantly on the move. I obey instructions and never let him cry. Then, at night, the others take over and I'm allowed to sleep in between night feedings. The baby thrives. He puts on a pound every week. We are all exhausted. We tell each other that this child is awake so much because he's so clever and so active and so alert. He is all those things but he's also a bloody nuisance and I am faced with the horrific thought that this might go on forever. He's my baby and I have to look after him. I start to hate him.

The cord between the baby and me has never been broken. I feel it tug at me during the night. I wake up suddenly and feel this pulling in my womb. A few minutes later the baby starts to cry and I know it's time for me to go and feed him. Sometimes I'm so tired I can't get up and I pretend that I haven't heard him cry. Then my husband nudges me. All I want is to lie there for just another five minutes. But he won't let me. He makes me get up and I hurl myself out of bed, declaring the unfairness of it all.

I reject my husband totally and, strangely enough, he doesn't seem to mind. He seems to identify with the child and always puts his son's needs first. I think he would like me to stay fused with my baby forever. We never go out, never enjoy ourselves. Our life is centred on this tiny, demanding child. I hate him and love him, feed him and want to murder him, dote on him and deliberately bump him in his pram. I am in chaos, constantly in tears, a weeping child trying to be a mother.

The only thing that is good is the feeding. At such times there is, between my son and me, a bond so pure, so flowing, so satisfying that neither he nor I need or want anything or anyone else. I long for feed times to last forever. I would sit for twenty-four hours a day with my nipple in his mouth, feeling him drain the warm milk from my swollen breasts. When he and I are fused, all is well. The moment the feeding is over, all is chaos and disorder.

I am lost in a world of milk and burps and dirty nappies and a baby who becomes glued to me, who I carry about for five months, borne with a mixture of pride and despair.

When he turns three months old I develop strange feelings of pins and needles and numbness in both hands. This is diagnosed as a swelling in the carpal tunnels of each hand and I am told to stop breast feeding my baby. I believe so strongly in the fact that I should give myself totally to my child that I refuse and as my hands become more and more painful I have to sleep each night with my hands resting in plaster casts. All this I endure willingly for the one union that binds me to my child. To wean him before he is ready is unthinkable.

When he is six months old we move to a beautiful, modern house. I am relieved to be alone with my husband and my son. I have to look after a house but the child can sit up now, play with toys, eat a rusk, roll around the floor. He still keeps us awake at night but the days seem more peaceful. He sleeps for three hours every morning. As soon as he goes to sleep I read a book. I wish he'd never wake up.

I develop a sense of guilt about housework. I hate it. I never do it properly. I keep telling myself that I'll do it properly next time. I never do. I feel trapped in my nice little house with my nice little baby. I never read a newspaper. What good is the news to me? There is no escape. Every day is endless and the same as the one before. There is no weekend for me. I never leave my son, never go anywhere without him, never have any sense of space.

When he stops waking to be fed at night he starts waking with teething problems. It is never-ending. He is six months old, eight months old, nine months old. I have not slept through one whole night since he was born.

I meet other women, living in the houses and streets nearby and we gather each afternoon at one another's homes and talk of babies and feeding and nappy rash. I would like to say that I find their conversation boring but that would be a lie. I need this kind of contact and I am grateful to have some-where pleasant to spend my afternoons. I watch the weather like a swagman, dreading rain. What will I do if I have to spend a whole day alone at home with my baby? The prospect is impossible to contemplate.

I keep ringing him up at work. It upsets him but I can't help it. I have to get rid of my anger and my despair on someone. If it's raining I ring him up to tell him it's raining and to ask him to tell me how to survive the day. He is bitingly calm, some-times helpful. I can't wait for him to get home not because I have missed him but because his presence will break the link between me and my child and set me momentarily free – if only to cook the dinner and wash the dishes.

He plays endlessly and delightedly with his son and as I listen to them chuckle and laugh I wonder why I, his mother, cannot play with him. I love him but he is, to me, a burden rather than a joy. Other mothers seem to enjoy their babies. Why can't I enjoy mine? He tells me I'm so unhappy because I'm intelligent and educated and I've written plays. He tells me I'll write again one day when my baby is bigger. I don't believe him. I know I'll never write again. I've become a vegetable.

Sex really disturbs me now. He wants my milk. He wants to be a baby, sucking milk from my breasts. I won't let him. It's my baby's milk. He becomes compulsive, insistent. I refuse. Finally he wins, as he always does, by patient persistence. He likes to lie sideways, his penis inside me, drinking milk while he makes love to me. It revolts and excites me. My emotions fragment. I am confused, I am mother, but he directs my mothering, demands it. There is, at this time, nothing in my life that I control.

Except my fantasies. I escape into a world of sexual fantasy. I fall in love with the chemist. He is dark and swarthy, handsome and exciting. I invent all kinds of reasons to go into his shop. Every man I meet becomes the sexual partner of my imaginings.

I am never parted from my son but when he is one year old I have to go into hospital for the much needed carpal tunnel operations on both wrists. My anxiety about leaving him is so great that I spend only one day in hospital and I come home weak and helpless but with our cord still safely intact. I live for months in this frustrating state of uselessness. I can't pin nappies properly; I can't use a knife; I keep dropping and breaking plates; I keep ringing my husband at work to tell him how awful everything is.

In the middle of all this we decide to have another child. As I can't even manage one child, I don't know what I'm doing contemplating another. I would like to say he talked me into it but he didn't. His wish to subdue me was no greater than my wish to be subdued.

I am heavy with pregnancy and very depressed. I can't stop eating so the doctor very kindly gives me some pills to take away my appetite. And then I do the strangest thing. We are driving along in the car and suddenly I open the door and I'm about to jump out. He has to reach across me and close the door and he slaps me across the face. Then I start to cry but I don't know why I'm crying. I think it's because I would have jumped out if he hadn't stopped me. I tell him I want to die. I don't want any more babies; I just want to die. I stop taking the appetite pills. I pretend to myself that it is the pills that have made me suicidal.

I grow enormous. I'm as wide as I am tall. This child inside me kicks me so hard that sometimes I fall onto the floor or find myself being propelled across the room. In my fantasy this is some monster that I'm growing inside me. I want a gentle girl but I can tell from the way he bashes me about that I won't get my wish. I hate this baby. I want to cut him out of me. My first-born is my one and only love. I am a dark cloud. I make everyone around me miserable.

And then he's born and I feel nothing. I don't even count his fingers and toes. All my thoughts are for the precious first child. I cannot tolerate our separation. The rules of the hospital are very strict and quite inhuman. They will not allow my son to visit me. My anxiety is so great that my husband agrees to bring him in and I will try to sneak downstairs to see him. A bitch of a sister catches me and makes me go back to my room. I look out of my third floor window and I see them down there. My husband is holding my son and my son is holding his teddy bear. I try to catch their attention. He looks up and cries, 'Mummy window! Mummy window!' He is satisfied. He smiles and waves. He has been told that he will see me and he has seen me. It is enough for him. It is not enough for me. My heart is breaking. I weep myself dry.

I am impatient to get home and when I do it is with a sense of relief and joy that I am restored to my first-born. He and I ignore this second child. We put it out in the garden to sleep, bring it in to feed it when it cries and then put it out again. Sometimes it gets dark before we remember that we have to bring it inside for the night. It's so good that we hardly know it exists. It never cries unless it's hungry, never has wind, never complains, never wants to be played with, sucks its thumb and actually sleeps through the night. I feel nothing for it at all – no love, no hate, no pleasure, no pain – nothing.

My first-born is two years old. He is clever and bright. He and I become friends. We laugh together, play together and, at certain times, attend to the new baby together. The new baby accepts it all. I feed him in noisy rooms and he becomes so accustomed to noise that he is unable to feed if it's quiet. For three or four months we lead a rather peaceful and happy existence.

Another reason for happiness is that my play is at last to be given a professional workshop production. For six weeks I work in rehearsal with the actors. The play is good. I can see it and feel it as they work with my script. And when the actual performance takes place, the audience obviously enjoys the play. It is a night of triumph for me. I can see the proof of my creative power there, up on stage. I cannot stop shaking. I feel that I am standing naked on stage. This should stimulate me to further creative effort, but it does not. I am lost in a world of physical creation. I cannot write at all.

The little boy who spends his day sleeping out of the garden suddenly springs to life. He is four and a half months old. He is kicking happily on the floor. Suddenly he flips himself over, then over again and he doesn't stop. He is an endless bundle of energy constantly flipping himself from one end of the house to the other. If he just flipped himself and did nothing else, then that would be alright but at every turn he comes across a book to tear up or a power point to stick his hand into or an electric cord to pull. I can't keep up with him. We have to childproof the whole house because he never learns anything. If he is reprimanded for turning on one power point, his mind cannot or will not make the leap to understand that it is wrong to turn on the next one.

We cannot take him anywhere. He poisons himself, raids cupboards, crawls onto the road. My nights become endless nightmares of different, horrible ways in which he dies. I keep hoping I can keep him alive until he's five, or maybe just until he's two. I cannot even leave him inside the house while I hang out the clothes. He has to be watched all the time. He exhausts me in a pure physical sense and when he starts to walk he becomes like a bull, charging into everything – aggressive, wild and free.

And then there is within me an extraordinary rush of love for this little person. It is as if he represents the angry part of me, the part I have never expressed, never set free. I love his aggression, smile at his bellowing cry. My spirit in him runs free.

We decide to have just one more child and by now I am quite pleased to think of myself as the mother of sons. Poor third baby – left to cry because there's too much to do to pick him up, ignored because the two other little boys take so much of my time. Not enough milk to feed him, not enough time to cuddle him. Slow to sit up, slow to crawl, slow to walk, slow to talk – because there's no time. One always has two hands, two sides, two parents - but where does the third child go? Whose hand does he hold? Which side of you does he sit on when the first two children have already established their rights? He must fight to get what love he can.

And what about me? Two were manageable. Three are impossible. I feel that I will never surface again. They are boisterous, exuberant, demanding. My day is an endless stream of appointed, domestic tasks. I've forgotten what it's like to read a book. I am vaguely aware that a Women's Liberation Movement has begun. But what has that got to do with me? I haven't the time to think about liberation. I'm the mother of three little boys.

I watch the man, my husband, watching me. He never helps me. He just watches. Every night he watches me get three little boys ready for bed, change them all into their pyjamas, put on all their nappies, give them their bottles of milk. His job is earning the money, mine is looking after the house. But I stop looking after the house. I don't do any housework. He complains. I ignore the complaints. I leave all the kitchen cupboards open so that he hits his head on them. He slams them closed. I leave them open. He tells me that ours is the only house in the neighbourhood with a garbage bin constantly on the front lawn. He has decided that it is his job to take out full garbage bins and mine to bring in empty ones. But I ignore the whole matter until he brings in the empty bin, swearing and cursing at me. He goes to mow the lawn and curses me again for the pegs that I leave all over the grass. It is supposed to be my job to weed the garden beds but I never do it. When the weeds look as if they are going to take over he pulls them out in angry frustration. He trips over the toys that the boys scatter from one end of the house to the other and berates me for my failure to clear them away.

It is a real battle now and I don't care. I deliberately burn his dinner. I think I like to get him angry. I'm so miserable myself that I want to make his life as unpleasant as possible. It's the only way I can express my aggression. If he comes home late I curse him. I tell him he has to come home at a reasonable hour to help me with the boys. Being a father is not as exciting as it used to be. Playing with his sons for about half an hour is all that he can take. He keeps escaping to the toilet with a newspaper. I never knew a man who could shit so much. He takes hours in the shower. I know he's just trying to get away from us and if there's no escape for me then why should there be one for him? The more he tries to escape, the angrier I become and the more I leave cupboard doors open and garbage bins out and burn his dinner.

He's right into big business now – Personnel Manager of big firm. I'm expected to be a Company wife at times and present myself at Company dinners. I hate this and make sure I look dowdy and never wear makeup.

We don't enjoy anything. Someone is always sick. They get tonsillitis and ear infections, measles, German measles, chicken-pox and mumps. I believe I'm immune to all these childhood illnesses but I'm not and I catch them all and suffer much more than the children do. Someone always needs an afternoon sleep or a morning sleep. We can never do anything and whenever we do go out, as a family, we never have any fun. I'm always angry with him or depressed because I eat too much and he is a gloomy, irritable man, angry with me for my shortcomings, irritated by the little boys who run about him and unable to tolerate their noise.

We both resent being parents and we take our resentment out on each other. We love our sons, but we hate the demands they make on us. My father and mother relieve us of our burdens every Saturday afternoon. All I want to do is read a book or to sit, absolutely quietly, doing nothing. He always wants to spend the time making love. I'm angry and he's angry and we are like cannibals, gnawing at each other's bones.

I hate him. I don't know that I hate him but I do. I hate him for going to work while I have to stay at home. I hate him for having somewhere to escape to when there's no escape for me. I hate him for stuffing me up with babies until little boys seem to be tumbling out of every corner of the house. I hate him for being reasonable. Beyond and above all else I hate him for being logical. I come to hate his male, mathematical, superficially, consciously logical mind. He tears me with logic at every turn. He demands that I explain my behaviour in his logical terms. But I can't. My logic is unconscious, not like his at all and I crumble under his biting analysis of my situation. He cannot hear my silent scream, my anguish, my despair. I am lost. I do not exist. 'What do you mean exactly,' he says. 'Define your terms.' How does one define despair? My intellect has been eaten away. He alone has survived.

He no longer stammers. He's cured. His verbal attacks are his substitute. He lacerates me instead of himself. I am his stammer. I am his affliction. I take it all. I have no boundaries, no barriers. I do not know how to protect myself. I am the easiest enemy to conquer. I want to be conquered. I long to be hurt. I am eager to be filled, to be drunk, to be swallowed. If he destroys me then he saves me from destroying others, and aids me in the destruction of myself. Perfect partners.

I hate him but I need him so I pretend to myself that I don't hate him. If ever he is late home from work I imagine that he has had a car accident and killed himself. When he arrives home

I smile to myself in relief, not because I'm glad he's home but because I haven't killed him. My wishes are not all powerful. Or I imagine that he gets killed and all the children get killed and then I'll be free and be a writer or go overseas or become a hermit.

Along with the fantasy of his death — either by accident or by some dread disease, goes the fantasy of the man I could really love. I think of the friend who killed himself and imagine what my life might be like now if I had chosen him. I imagine that the chemist tells me he loves me and takes me away to a new life. I imagine that some rich millionaire falls in love with me and sweeps me away to a life of peace and luxury forever. Half my waking time is spent on sexual fantasy. It relieves the monotony while I'm cooking dinner or changing nappies or walking down the street with my sons.

He hates my mess. If ever we have visitors he runs around putting everything away. By the time he's finished it looks as if no one lives here. I don't co-operate. I like toys on the floor and Vegemite on the chairs. It seems more friendly that way. And what's the point of cleaning up?

I hate my life. I want every day to be over. I long to sleep. In four years I have not had one whole night of sleep. I constantly cry over what could have been. I look back and see myself at twenty-four — three play written, slim, alive, ready to face the world. I wallow in a sense of tragic loss. I imagine all the plays I would have written if I had taken the other path. I know that it is too late for me now. I'm thirty-one years old, my creativity wasted, my vitality gone. He tells me that I enjoy all this suffering. He's right but he does not see, and nor do I, that he plays my perfect counterpart for he plays so subtly, so cunningly that even he is not aware of the role he takes. I certainly never see his need to control blending with my need to be controlled; his desire to destroy moulded to my desire for destruction. All I know and see is that I'm sinking and he's surviving. He has grown strong and firm and sure; I have withered and died. I cannot breathe. My annihilation is complete.

I lie listlessly in my London bed and look out at the grey mid-morning sky. I cannot move. Nine years and three thousand miles separate me from the man and yet he invades me still.

SEVEN

It is my last day in London. I should get up and do all the things that I haven't done. I should take a look at the Tower of London, watch the changing of the guards at Buckingham Palace, go to Westminster Abbey. But I can't move. I've melted into the bedclothes. And what am I doing here, on the other side of the world, lost and naked in a strange hotel bed? I am absolutely alone. There's no one to save me here. No one to pull me out of my despair the way he did, nine years ago.

I am thirty-one years old and I am defeated. He looks at me and he sees that I've sunk so far down that I might actually drown so he sets about saving me. He sits me down and he tells me that what I need is an outside interest. I need to work again, part-time. I need to get my mind and my intellect going again. He thinks that if I can get out of the house, teach, meet people – then I might be able to write again. We both know that writing is the only thing that can save me and we do something constructive about achieving that goal.

It is as if he has opened my cage. We both know that he longs to keep me there, his little bird safely locked away from the outside world. I have wanted my imprisonment just as much as he has wanted to keep me imprisoned but we both realize that it hasn't worked. I'm so unhappy that he gets no pleasure from me and he sees that I have forgotten how to sing.

But his attempt to liberate me is an unspoken admission of guilt, a kind of realization that he has contributed to my self-destruction and he sees that if he turns the key then I will, somehow, be able to open the door and let myself out.

The first result is an extraordinary upsurge in my sexuality. I am openly, wantonly sexual for the first time in my marriage.

I can't wait for him to get home at night. I want to make love to him; even take the initiative. He can't believe it. I make an enormous effort to get slim again and succeed in doing so. I have an operation that removes the ugly, painful varicose veins from my legs. And we become close now, this husband and I. It's as if he's put me on the wheel of fire and now I've come full circle. I've paid enough for whatever nameless crime I've committed. Expiation complete. He sets me free.

I am teaching now for two hours a week. The first thing I buy is freedom from drudgery. I spend all I earn on having the children minded and the housework done one day a week. He helps me with my work. I'm teaching English to a class of Personnel Management students and he provides me with ideas, material, letters, reports. I am very grateful for the guidance he gives me. I find it very strange to be teaching Technical English. The precise, objective language of business letters and reports is alien to me. I am at a loss to understand how an Honours degree in English Literature should be seen to qualify me for such teaching but I am glad to be working and spend a great deal of time preparing my lessons. He even goes over the students' work that I have marked and shows me how I might have done it better. I don't resent this. I know he's better equipped to teach this subject than I am. He has a precise vocabulary; his spelling is faultless; his sentence structure superb.

Then I am offered one more hour's work, at night, and I'm not sure whether to take it. He sees that work is good for me and encourages me to take the extra hour, offering to mind the children while I teach. I'm hesitant because it is a class of Electrical Engineering students and I won't be able to use the material he provides me with. I'll have to devise my own. He boosts my confidence, though, and I decide I can handle it.

I enter the classroom on the first night. There are about fifteen young men in the room. I feel a kind of terror in the pit of my stomach, a feeling I am always to experience on first meeting a class. I am very slim at the moment and mini-skirts are in and mine is so short that you can almost see my pants. At least I can feel good about my appearance.

I am ready to give my carefully prepared lesson on the need to be objective in technical and scientific writing. There's a man sitting in the front row. He's skinny, with white skin, a big, broad forehead, frizzy black hair, thick horn-rimmed spectacles, prominent white teeth, thick lips. I notice him for two reasons; firstly, he's so ugly and secondly, he's obviously foreign and has isolated himself from the more Australian members of the class. After an initial nervousness, I proceed quite confidently to give my lesson. I know that what I am saying is right. After about ten minutes the man in the front stops me. In halting English that is very difficult to understand he tells me that I am talking rubbish. How can I possibly say that a technical or scientific writer should not use the pronouns 'I' and 'me'? Haven't I ever heard of Freud? Do I imagine for one moment that Freud, the greatest scientific writer of our age, could have written his work without a basically subjective approach?

I start to argue with him. I try to tell him I'm not talking about Freud, I'm talking about describing machines and systems and writing technical reports. He won't stop arguing with me. I don't know what to do. Everyone else is bored, not just bored but hostile towards the man in the front row. It's my first night and they're willing to give me a go. He's not. He catches me on the use of particular words and phrases. He makes me feel unsure of myself and I don't know how to deal with the situation. After ten minutes of fruitless argument I ask him to see me after the class and try to get on with my lesson. I go back to my prepared material and continue as if his discussion with me has not occurred. But I feel very shaken and I can't hide this fact from myself. Perhaps he is right. He sits there, looking hostile. The others take down notes I dictate on the steps one should follow in writing a technical description. He writes nothing down. He plays with his pen, moving it about in his fingers, as if he needs something to distract him to fill in the time. The look on his face is cynical. I can feel that he considers himself to be far more intelligent than I am. Nothing I might say could possibly be worth his while writing down. I realize I have a problem and I'm not sure how I'm going to handle it.

The hour is over. I feel relieved. I know I've given my prepared lesson well. One nice, smiley, Australian boy comes out to me as he leaves the class. 'I'm going to enjoy your lessons,' he says. I feel reassured and warmed by his praise. I feel that his response represents the feeling of all the members of the class, except for this monster in the front row.

They all leave – all except him. He looks sheepish as he comes out, almost embarrassed. His diffidence makes me feel more confident. 'Look,' I say, 'I have to get home now. My husband is expecting me. But next week I'll stay after class and we can continue our discussion.' He smiles at me. A strange smile, one that I cannot put into any category. He is very polite; he agrees. He says he will look forward to arguing with me. He leaves. I go home.

I tell my husband about it, because I always tell my husband everything. I need to tell him why I will be late the following week. He doesn't mind. Whatever I might want to do, however I might want to extend myself in my teaching is alright with him.

I don't know why but I can't get this strange man out of my mind. I keep rehearsing what I will say to him, prepare word for word my defence of the way I am teaching. I go over and over it. His face keeps appearing – his challenge, my feeling that he is mocking me.

The week goes by and I return to the classroom but he's not there. I'm appalled. I feel insulted. How dare he treat me like this? What rudeness! His absence expresses his indifference. I am indignant, furious, disappointed. The class proceeds peacefully though, because he is not there. At the end of the hour I tell the class that I will test them the following week by giving them a technical description to write in class.

I try to forget the man but I can't. I'm full of anger. I feel that he has belittled me. I hope he'll never come back. I hope he will come back. The next week he is there, smiling at me, as if he hasn't been away at all. I give them the written test to do and wonder if he'll do it or if he'll just sit there as if anything I might ask the class to do could not be relevant to him. I am surprised. He attempts the test, even appears to put great effort and concentration into it. The test takes the full hour. I sit there, trying to work, but my eyes keep travelling to his face, his long white fingers, his thick, protruding lips, the glasses that slip down on his nose. I feel an almost eager anticipation of the discussion we will have. My stomach is fluttering. I feel quite shaky. I don't know why.

At the end of the hour, the smiling, friendly Australian talks to me. He's very nice and quite handsome. I feel a responding warmth and smile. They all leave, except for the man in the front.

'Would you like coffee with me?' he asks. I agree and feel an immediate sense of guilt. I am married with three sons. I am not supposed to go and drink coffee with students. My morality tells me that this is wrong – but I go just the same.

On the way to the coffee shop I question him. 'Where do you come from?'

'Lebanon,' he replies.

I don't think before I respond. 'If we lived on the other side of the world we might be killing each other,' I say, actually laughing. Then I realize, too late, that this is not a laughing matter.

'Are you a Jew?' he asks.

'Yes,' I reply. We both adjust ourselves to this feeling of hereditary enmity while we walk in silence to the coffee shop. Will he jump on me and slit my throat on the way? He doesn't. He is passive, quiet.

We sit down and I can feel excitement mounting up inside me. There is, I realize, something in me that longs to allow my whole self to bubble out for this man. I feel a compulsive urge to explain myself to him, to allow him to see what I am. I resist the compulsion to speak and instead ask him about himself. I ask him why he's come to Australia. His answer astounds me. He tells me he's come here because he wants to read all of Chomsky's works. He needs to read these in English and they're not available in English in Lebanon. Is he joking? I must have a bewildered look on my face. 'You know Chomsky's work, don't you?' he asks. I shake a negative. He is now the one to be shocked. How can I call myself an English teacher if I've never read Chomsky? He is appalled at my ignorance.

'I've read the whole of Freud,' I reply, in some attempt to raise myself from the level of ignoramus. He's happy about that and starts to discuss Freud's theories. He seems to be quite pleased with my knowledge. I watch myself rise in his estimation. It's terribly important to me that he should not think I'm dumb. Half an hour has gone by without my realizing it. I look at my watch and tell him I will have to go; if I'm any more than half an hour late my husband will be angry. 'He's jealous, ' I say, 'and won't believe I've just been talking.'

'Aren't you free to please yourself?' he asks. His eyes mock me. No. No, I'm not free. The man I'm married to would not tolerate infidelity, even on the level of my talking with this man. I am ashamed of my bondage. He sees it in my face.

'You must liberate yourself,' he says, gently. I rush away, confused, flushed, unsure – dash home to where everything is safe, known, understood. He asks me why I'm late. I tell him that the student I had previously mentioned had turned up this week and I had stayed to talk to him, as arranged. I do not mention the coffee or that a strange man has told me that I must set myself free.

I am impatient for the next week, for the after-class coffee, for the talk. For the next six weeks we talk the brief half hours away. I learn that he is not just a Freudian; he is a Marxist, a real, idealistic Communist. I argue against him from my middle class, bourgeois, individualistic concept of existence. I tell him that I would not like to live in a Communist country, that I value being free. It is the first time that anyone has made me think about whether or not I am free. He suggests to me that I am a slave of materialism, capitalism, environment and the roles my society expects me to play. I have never had my basic values challenged before but I am ripe for it. I am one of the oppressed. I am ready for revolution. All I need is his prodding to set me on my way.

I keep quiet about him at home. I long to talk about him but I don't dare. I know why I don't dare. I intend to have an affair with him. It is not something that I think might happen. It is something that I am going to make happen. I see in the Arab a vehicle for my liberation, a tool by which I might be set free to write again. But, if I am honest, it is more than that. I like the fact that he is an Arab and a Communist, both a racial and ideological enemy. To be even more honest, it is a consciously decided upon act of rebellion against my husband who has kept me trapped for seven years. I want to rebel in the way that will hurt him the most. The way I feel about this Arab makes me think I've been cheated all those years. My husband has constantly made me feel that I am inadequate as a woman, that I have an abnormally low level of sexual desire. Now I want this strange man so much I could gobble him up. I feel insatiable; a powerful sexual urge drives me on. All my fantasies culminate in a fixed sexual concentration on the Arab.

I am the teacher and he is the pupil. I am thirty-one and he is twenty-four. I take the initiative. I know that he wants me as much as I want him. I know he respects me. I know that he will not ask me, but I also know that if I suggest a relationship he will agree. He is like a little child when I make my wishes clear to him. He can't believe his luck. He feels alien and isolated in this country. He has been used to a high degree of mental stimulation. His language difficulties and the sort of people he is forced to meet and work with in Australia, make this country seem like an intellectual wasteland to him. His talks with me are the only ones he has on an intellectual level with an English-speaking person. He is afraid to approach Australian girls, doesn't know how to talk to them. He has not been with woman since his arrival in Australia six months before. He is hungry for sex. I know exactly how to do it. I plot and plan the whole thing. I am totally in control. I dominate this relationship. I am determined to control it all the way. My husband is due to go away on a week's business trip and I plan the seduction to coincide with his absence. It works exactly according to plan.

It is real betrayal that I plan. He is to come to my house, to make love in my marital bed. I feel no guilt. I feel that I am dishing out a well-deserved punishment. I need to act it out.

He arrives. I feel impatient, yet in control. The boys are all asleep and I don't expect them to wake up. I realize, as soon as he starts to make love to me, that he's had almost no experience. He comes straight way; he can't wait at all. I feel frustrated but I like his innocence. He makes love to me five times in two hours and each time he wants me so much that he can't wait. He is in despair. He thinks that there is something wrong with him. This time I don't panic. I'm perfectly calm and I know exactly what to do. He tells me that he's very inexperienced and he asks me to teach him all I know about making love.

I tell him that the next night we should eat together and have a bottle of wine before we attempt to make love. He agrees to anything I suggest. I start to get the feeling that he would do anything I ask. I delight in this reversal, to be the master instead of the slave.

The next night he arrives. We eat and drink and talk and then make love. This time he is able to wait and I teach him with my body the way to make love to me. This time I control and I work towards orgasm and I climax with a shattering force that leaves me shaking, weeping, laughing. I can tell from his face that no woman has ever come like that with him before and the power of my coming is so great that I believe I have achieved something quite extraordinary. And so it begins for both of us at this instant. We are cunt and prick, man and woman, mutually yearning, equally giving, flying for the first time to the stars, to the moon. We roll about the heavens, strive for and sometimes touch the sun – rising, falling, burning, cooling. 'Lie on my heart,' he says. And I lie on him, in the quiet after time, heartbeats joined in the oneness of our giving.

What is it – to love an enemy? 'We are,' he says, in his hesitant but metaphoric English, 'like two lamps whose shadows overlap momentarily.' And indeed we are. What can I say? How can I express it? – the poignant realization that you hold, curled in your being, a precious and delicate spring of loving – so fragile because you know from the beginning that it is a love that can never be fully realized, never shown to the world, never exhibited, never flaunted, never shouted from the mountain tops; a love that must remain secret, enclosed, contained within; a love full of wonder where joy is constantly tempered by sadness, laughter tinged with tears. A love that begins with the full knowledge that it must end is surely more precious than a love one can imagine going on forever. It is exquisite. It is perfection. It is fantasy brought into the realm of reality. It is the thing that dreams are made of. It is love.

It is because we are enemies that our love is so special. To me all Arabs are ignorant, primitive, cowardly. To him all Jews are vicious killers who drink the blood of their victims. Centuries of hatred, prejudice, misinformation are ingrained in our brains. And yet we love. There is for me, and I think for him, a real challenge in proving that an Arab and a Jew can come together and find, between them, an area of peace.

He becomes my obsession. I can think of nothing else. I live and breathe only for the moments I am with him. I go to sleep with his face crowding my consciousness and I wake to find him still flooding my thoughts. I think of him all day – while I am driving the car, washing the nappies, cooking the dinner.

I think of him while my husband is making love to me. He is my other life, the world I escape to in my imaginings.

I spend three hours with him each week. They are the only three hours that seem real. We squash a lifetime into three hours. I drive to his place. He lives in a room in a house in Strathfield. Not a nice house, not a nice room. It doesn't matter. The setting is immaterial. We have both waited all week for this one meeting. I feel almost sick with wanting him by the time I get there. When I arrive we cannot even say 'Hello' to each other. We can only hug and kiss and make love. To touch him is to come home. To feel his skin next to mine is like returning to the place where I belong. To feel him locked inside me – to kiss, to hug, to move, to hold, to fly, to come – counterpoints of harmony, measuring our oneness.

The first hunger satisfied, the second need asserts itself – the eagerness to talk. In lovemaking I teach. In the world of ideas it is he who takes the lead. I love to listen to him talk. He is a man of metaphors, struggling always to find the right image in which to express his thoughts, his ideas, his love. He plies me with literature to read – Marx, Fromm, Chomsky, Levi-Strauss. He expects me to discuss these works with him. They overwhelm me. I don't really understand them. He makes me feel I'm nowhere near as clever as he is. I'd rather listen to him talk. He explains them all to me, in simple terms that I can understand and once I've grasped the ideas I am able to discuss them with him. Then we make love again, then talk again, make love again.

I know he's cleverer than I am because he understands all these books and I don't. I admire his intellect. And I admire his idealism. He's prepared to die for his beliefs. It's the first time I've known a human being who puts the welfare of his people before his own. He believes in the possibility of a Communist world, of equality for all, of genuine love of man for man. He does not believe in violence or hatred or war. He dissociates himself from terrorism as a valid mode of behaviour. But he teaches me to understand the plight of the Arabs, makes me realize why they have felt a need to resort to terrorist activities. He gives me long lectures on the state of affairs in the Middle East. He puts everything into objective, historical perspective for me. He shows me the other side.

I would, however, rather make love than talk and he accuses me often of being nothing but my cunt. But he knows that he is also, at this time, bound by his sexual need of me. There is, however, a difference. He sees sexuality as something he would one day like to be free of. To him it is limiting. I see sexuality as something I would like to indulge in and get lost in forever.

There are deep, essential differences. I remain primarily inward turned and individualistic. I flirt with Marxism but am never converted. The idea of putting the welfare of others before my own is alien to me as is the idea of sharing with others. I like to own things. I cannot take the step he would like me to take. He sees himself, in terms of evolution, as more highly civilized than I am because he is able to take that step beyond self to the idealistic concern for others. I see him as more primitive than I am. He has no table manners. He eats with his hands. I can't imagine him at a dinner party. On the level of social behaviour he is, to me, the primitive Arab. He feels that he has broken away from his upbringing and his environment and that this entitles him to regard himself as free. But I don't agree with him. I see that he is a fanatic, a slave to his ideals, as bound to them as any man might be bound to his religious beliefs. To me, he is not free. We argue these points constantly, until the argument becomes too aggressive and we resolve our differences by making love.

His ideological beliefs commit him to regarding women as his equals. To him this is not just theory. He really sees me and treats me as his equal and this carries over into his lovemaking. I never feel that he takes me, only that he joins me. My husband, whose lovemaking is gentle, sensuous, varied, technically perfect can only climax on top of me so that I always end up feeling as if I've been ravished, raped, mastered. The Arab can come anyhow - on top, underneath, sideways, upside down; it doesn't matter to him and his coming is never accompanied by the hammering thrusts that are characteristic of my husband. Instead he stops still, ceases to move at all, so that his coming is an exquisite, delicate, throbbing gift that he lovingly presents to me.

I enjoy the stolen, precious hours I spend with my lover but find it very difficult to manage at home. I do not want my husband to touch me. I become cold, unloving, frigid, uncooperative.

In the beginning I say nothing about my Arab friend but now I keep talking about him, not as a sexual object but as a source of intellectual stimulation. I read a lot of Marxist literature and constantly try out my half-read, half-digested ideas on my husband. My grasp of the material is so poor that I fall victim to his biting logic every time. I seem to be attacked on both sides and my failure reinforces the idea that, on an intellectual level, I cannot compete with these men. I long to be writing again, to find my own, innate, feminine way – a way that these two clever men would regard as unintelligent and chaotic; a way that I know is a real, though unconscious, road to truth. I am bombarded by male logic. My path is eaten away by their pressure.

I dream the dream of the mountain. There is a large granite rock blocking the track along which my train is supposed to run. I cannot seem to find any way to get through this enormous mountain. It is both husband and lover who block my way. They are both the mountain. My head shatters and splits as I collide with their unyielding surface, my brains splattered like entrails, pouring in a bloody mess onto the ground. Why? Why can I never find my own way? Why am I always losing myself in someone else's journey? Why don't I have the courage to venture out on my own? Why do I constantly relinquish any sense of self in order to share my train trip with a man?

I am definitely not managing. Anyone can see that. I've put on a stone in four weeks. It is the guilt that I cannot handle. Infidelity is wrong. I am sure that my husband knows. He knows because he is Superman and he has X-ray vision. He can see inside my soul, I can tell that he can tell that I'm being unfaithful to him.

The Arab tries to help. He tells me that fidelity is meaningless and that everyone should live in communes and practice free love. His comments seem irrelevant. He makes his position quite clear. He loves me. He tells me that I am to him like Solomon's ring, the magic source of power that will give to a man all that his heart desires. He loves me, but he will never play a part in the breaking up of my marriage. My place, he says, is with my husband and with my children. I do not, he feels, have the right to smash up my family unit.

But I want to smash it up. I want to get an axe and chop up the whole thing. That is something the Arab cannot see – how great and deep and wide is my horrific need to chop up my husband into a thousand little pieces. The desire to destroy my husband becomes a compulsion. I want to tell him that I am in love with another man. I want to see what will happen to him when I tell him. I want to see if I can shatter his calm hold on life. The words keep bubbling up into my mouth and I keep swallowing them down.

I don't like the game that I am playing but I play it all the same. It is necessary. The compulsion to confess finally over-powers me and I can't hold it back any longer and I blurt out the fact that I'm in love with someone else and then I stand back and watch what my revelation does to him. I am astounded by my power, staggered by my realization that I can destroy this man if I want to. He breaks down, crumbles before me. First of all he confesses that once, on a business trip to New Zealand, he had deliberately slept with another woman. This was, he tells me, his way of taking revenge on me for my infidelity with my dead university friend. Having made his confession, he then breaks down completely and weeps like a child and tells me that he could cope with my having a casual sexual relationship of the kind he had indulged in, but that my saying that I loved the Arab was impossible for him to tolerate.

I'm not sure what to do. I tell him that I want to go away with my lover for just one weekend and that I will then end the relationship. I almost believe what I'm saying. As I look at him, broken down, I realize that I need him to remain strong. If he breaks down the whole world will fall apart. If anyone is going to have a breakdown, I want it to be me.

So I go away for the weekend with my Arab but it is not the idyllic, loving time I have envisaged. My guilt is too great to enable me to enjoy myself. My confession to my husband has marred the joy of being with my lover. He feels it too. Our shadows cease to overlap. We retreat to our separate, antagonistic selves. We fight and argue and hate each other so much that I really think it is all over. The hostility that exists between us cannot be bridged. He cannot understand why I've told my husband. He sees me as a destructive woman that he could well do without. In tears I leave him near his home and drive off. I don't care what happens to me. I come to a busy intersection and don't even bother to look to my right. I just keep driving and smash into the first car that gets in my way. I'm not badly hurt but I'm very shaken and the car's a mess and all I want is to get home to my husband and children. I want to confess; I want to be forgiven; I want to promise to be good; I want to tell him that I love him and that I'll never, never be bad again.

He forgives me and my symbolic smashing of myself in the car frightens me so much that I really believe I have come to terms with myself. I can see now that my place in the world is with my husband and with my children. I have made my gesture; I have rebelled against him, proved that I can destroy him if I want to but only, it seems, by also destroying myself. Suddenly I want to keep intact what little there is left of me. I want to get back into my cage. Imprisonment seems attractive now. Certainly it is safe.

A week later the Arab rings me up just to see if I am alright. Then we are weeping into the phone and we almost climax by telepathy. And then I know that a relationship that might have begun as an act of revolution has become, for both of us, a passion that, like the unfolding of a Greek tragedy, must be acted out to its inevitable conclusion.

There begins for me, now, a time of terror. My fear is that of being found out. I start to pray to God, an extraordinary thing to do considering that I ceased believing in him so long ago.

As I drive to my lover's house I pray to God to let me have just this one day, to not be seen by anyone, to not be found out, to not let the car break down, to not let me have an accident. My prayers seem to be answered.

So precious are our times together that each is lived as if it will be the last. So strongly do we feel that the outside world will prevent our love that it is with a renewed sense of wonder that we come together again each week. It is a time of loving that is characterized by sadness rather than joy for now, indeed, we both long for a life together and both know that this is impossible.

Then it happens – inexplicably, unexpectedly. I am pregnant. I have an intra-uterine device that is supposed to make pregnancy impossible. None the less, I am pregnant.

I'm not sure what to do. My husband even feels guilty, as if it's his fault. This makes me feel worse. I tell my parents. They ask me to come and see them. My mother tells me that three children are enough, that the boys will suffer and be deprived if I have a fourth child. Our house is only big enough for three children. My father does not take part in this conversation. I don't really know how he feels about it. My mother is sure that I should have an abortion.

My husband doesn't want any more children. He's always wanted a girl but a fourth child, boy or girl, would be an emotional and financial drain. But, he says, the decision must be mine. He will give me absolute and total support, whatever I should decide. I'm sure I'll have an abortion. It seems the only sensible decision to make. How could I possibly manage a pregnancy not knowing who fathered my child.

When I tell my Arab lover I am sure that he will also want me to have an abortion. As we lie there, making love, talking, we both realize that perhaps the animosity with which our peoples have killed each other for centuries might somehow be resolved by the implanting of an Arab-Jewish child in my womb. We start to feel that what has happened transcends both him and me and our individual needs and differences, that the child in my womb must be allowed to live. And then I am overcome with a longing for the child to be his and I decide that, whatever the personal cost, I will nourish and nurture and give birth to this child.

I realize fairly soon that I've made a mistake. The pregnancy creates intolerable tensions and I become a helpless child. Now that I've decided not to have an abortion, my parents and my husband support me wholeheartedly. The three of them get stuck into the awful business of getting us a bigger house. I don't want to move, refuse to co-operate, tell them I might have a miscarriage. My father produces $9,000 to allow us to bridge the gap between the price we'll get for our old house and cost of a new one. I don't want to move. I keep crying. They all think it's just the prospect of a fourth child that's making me weep. They think I'm very brave to be going through with it. They admire me for refusing to take the easy way out and have my unborn child disposed of. I am constantly aware of their moral, physical, financial support.

The thing inside me takes on the aspects of a monster. I am sure it will be deformed, ugly, sub-normal, or have three eyes. Maybe it will even be black. The crime I am committing is, to me, gross and unforgivable. To be unfaithful and to flaunt one's infidelity by producing another man's child is, surely, the ultimate act of betrayal. It seems so to me.

But once a week, in the magic of my other life, lying beside my Arab, my lover, feeling his love as he lays his head on the unborn child – I know and again know that what I am doing is right.

As soon as it starts to become obvious that I am pregnant he will no longer allow me to come to his room. What will people think, he wants to know, if they see a pregnant woman come to his room. His rejection shocks me. I berate him. It could, after all, be his child. How can he be ashamed of me? But he is ashamed of me. I turn up at his room despite his insistence that I should not come. He is horrified. I accuse him of being primitive, uncivilized and totally insensitive to my needs. Doesn't he understand that now, at this moment, I need his love and support? No. Apparently he doesn't understand that at all. Or has the horror of what we are doing come home to him too? He tries a new approach. He says he's been to a doctor and had tests done that prove him to be sterile. Is he serious? I don't know. I'm hysterical. I don't believe him. He can't handle my hysteria. He insists that the child is my husband's. He is positive that he has nothing to do with my pregnancy. He forbids me to come to his house again.

I come again the next week but he's not there. I'm furious. I refuse to be abandoned in this way. He rings and tells me that he's moved and that he won't give me his new address. I hate him now, with a terrible fierceness. I long to cut his child out of me but it's too late – it's growing and kicking and moving. I am sick with terror. I feel now a victim, trapped, seduced, forced to see to conclusion something that I have come to abhor.

I cannot stop eating. I cry all the time. Veins burst out all over my legs. One terrible varicose vein extends from my thigh, across my groin, causing one side of the labia to hang down an inch, throbbing with a heavy, pulsing pain. I can't seem to sit or stand. I'm sure I'm going to die.

Now that my lover has abandoned me I start to hope that the child will be my husband's. My husband feels responsible for my pregnancy and his guilt is so great that he is kinder to me than he has ever been before. He hates to see me endure the real physical pain that seems to accompany this pregnancy from beginning to end. The physical aspects are obvious, the mental anguish I must keep to myself.

I am still teaching part-time, still have three little boys to look after, still have to cook dinner and carry out the endless domestic tasks that inevitably have to be attended to. This keeps me in touch with some kind of reality. Without these touchstones the insanity inside me would erupt without control.

The Arab rings me a few weeks before the birth. He gives me his address and asks me to let him know when the baby is born. I shout obscenities into the telephone. My hatred of him is dull and hard.

The tension mounts in me. I become enormous, swollen with baby and fluid and veins. The pregnancy becomes intolerable, the mental torment unendurable. I beg for hospitalization and ask for the birth to be induced.

The baby is turned the wrong way. It is a long and painful labour. I accept injections, take drugs, inhale gas – anything. I have no control. I am beyond all help. I want the doctor to do a Caesarian but he refuses. I have to wait for the baby to turn around. It is like waiting for death. Finally the baby turns and I step outside myself to watch myself give it birth. I cannot accept the responsibility of having anything to do with it.

He gives me my daughter and I look at her and see the Arab's face look back at me and all the hysteria of the last nine months breaks out of my mouth and they all smile at my response – they think I'm overcome with the joy of giving birth to a girl after three boys. How will I ever explain her extraordinary face?

I dread the arrival of my husband. He comes, ecstatic, over-joyed. 'You've made my life complete,' he says. 'You've given me the daughter I've so longed for.' But what about her face? He doesn't seem to notice anything strange about her face. She is his daughter. But what about everyone else? Won't they notice how different she is? There's something about her that's like my brother's oldest girl. I cling onto that sliver of likeness. I play it up, point it out. Then I remember that my oldest son is also unlike anyone – unusual, different. Does it really matter?

I have her photograph taken in the hospital and send it to the Arab out of spite. I hope it will hurt him. He rings me at the hospital. 'She's mine.' He says, suddenly full of tender feeling for me. I abuse him, swear at him.

The tension of the first few weeks subsides, especially as I do not seem to have been found out. When I bring my daughter home it is, truly, a time of happiness for us all. She makes such a difference, this little baby girl. We dote on her, adore her, spoil her. She is a princess.

The Arab rings me again. Why do I agree to see him? Why don't I grasp onto and hold and keep the contentment I now feel with husband, sons, daughter? Why do I so willingly plunge myself into almost certain self-destruction, so consciously destroy not only myself but the things I hold dear? I don't know. Maybe I love the Arab. Do I? He begs and pleads. He loves me and longs for me. I cannot excuse or explain or understand his rejection of me during pregnancy. Nor can I resist his present plea for love.

She is six weeks old when we go to see him. She has changed, grown more like my family. He looks at her. 'She's not mine,' he says. 'She's beautiful, but she's not mine.' I don't know whose she is but I want to convince the Arab that she belongs to him. He's not sure what to think. He both wants and doesn't want her to be his. I decide, in my own mind, that she doesn't belong to either of them. She is mine, mine alone. She becomes my world. I love her with fierce affection.

The Arab makes love to me and I am trapped again in the world of our passion. I tell my lover that I want to live with him, that I want to end my marriage and spend my life with him. Why do I play this game? I don't really mean it. I just want to break him down, want to reduce him to grovelling before me, want him to offer me a life with him. He refuses to play my game. He goes on refusing. I go on insisting, but I don't know why I do. I know that if he asked me to leave my family I wouldn't do it, yet I continue to behave as if that is the thing I want to do.

In the end the Arab is terrified of me. He sees me as a woman bent on self-destruction and ready to drag him along with me. He does the only thing that seems reasonable for him to do. He returns to Lebanon.

The minute he leaves I pull myself together. I stop crying and stop stuffing myself with food, calm down, wean the baby, go back to work and find that life is perfectly easy to deal with. I'm still in love with the Arab, crave him sexually, need him, want him, long for him but now that he's removed himself from my physical presence, he's somehow put himself back where he rightly belongs – in the realm of my fantasies. He is the first man who has made the physical reality of sex a better thing than my imagination could conjure up. Now that he's gone I can live with him constantly in my mind, his passion imprinted in me, relived each day in imagined ecstasy.

And I start to write – not plays or poems or stories, but letters – long impassioned love letters to my Arab far away. I imagine him, dressed in traditional Arab garb, flying on his magic carpet, penis erect, winging his way to me. My love becomes refined by imagining. The everyday life of wife, mother, teacher are secondary to the life I live in the innermost recesses of my quiet, dark womb.

My husband now decides to get out of the business world and to become a teacher. This pleases me, even though he will earn less money and it means that it is now financially necessary for me to teach full-time. I am surprised that anyone should give a full-time teaching job to the mother of four small children so I take my work seriously and put a lot of effort into it.

I decide to liberate myself. I've been reading Simone de Beauvoir and Kate Millet and Germaine Greer and I'm starting to believe that I've a right to be free of domestic bondage. I attend one meeting of the Women's Liberation Movement and one Women's Electoral Lobby meeting. On both occasions I am aware of my own reluctance to join in group activity. If I'm going to be liberated, I'll just have to do it on my own.

I'm ready to rebel but, as usual, my husband is three steps ahead of me. He anticipates my rebellion and offers to take over his share of domestic burdens. He doesn't let me shout and scream and declare that I won't run around after him and do everything while he sits on his arse and watches me. He does his share. He takes over the family washing, an enormous task with two boys wetting the bed and one child in nappies. I make breakfast and leave for work and he gets the kids ready for school, kindergarten, baby-sitter. If he wants a cup of tea he starts making it for himself instead of expecting me to do it.

But I still do much more around the house than he does and he still fills me with resentment. I still hate the three times a week sexual battles, still spend most nights sleeping on the lounge, still feel eaten away, put upon, cheated. Work is important. It is an escape. But I still hate him. I wish he were dead. I don't realize how strong that wish is until, one night, I find myself taking our car down the steep driveway to put it away in the garage. He is standing in the garage and I go to put my foot on the brake to stop the car but I can't find the brake at all. My foot keeps going onto the accelerator. I shout out to him and he gets out of the way just in time and I crash the car through the boxes of rubbish at the end of the garage and smash into the fibro wall before I can bring the car to a halt.

He is very shaken. So am I. I have nearly killed him. It is frightening to have to face such obvious proof of my wish to murder him.

He constantly picks at me, criticizes me, wants to cut down any new thoughts I might have. Always logical, always calm, always demanding a reasonable rather than an emotional response. My spirit is crushed. I wilt under his critical glare. I feel he's always looking to see if he can find something wrong with the way I've washed the dishes, or cooked the dinner. He even criticizes the way I teach. He is so tired of my inadequacies and my complaints and I don't blame him. I couldn't possibly live with someone like me. It's a source of wonder to me that he puts up with me at all.

Am I just testing him? Am I like the naughty child, trying to estimate how much its mother is prepared to take? Will she still love me if I do this or that awful thing? My own mother opted out. She couldn't deal with my aggressive, murderous rage. Can he? I think I'm putting this husband-mother to the supreme test. And that, I think, is why I blurt it all out – scream it at him, one hot summer night; spit the truth at him – the Arab, the continuing affair, the fact that he may not be my baby's father.

I despise what I am doing but a terrible need compels me to confess. It has something to do with self-preservation. It is hitting back, with one vicious blow, for the years of day by day gnawing away at my essence. I long to emerge from my wilderness, to be resurrected, to be whole. But he can snuff me with a word and so I use the last trick that I have. It is dirt I throw and mud I sling but it's the only thing I have left to fight with. The fact that I've kept this monstrous secret for two years is proof to him that there is an area of me that he can't get at and can't control. And so my telling has about it the feeling of a battle for survival.

Rebellion makes no sense to me unless I can throw it in someone's face and he, like my mother, always backs down when faced with real aggression. I want him to fight back, because she did not fight back. I want him to throw me out, reject me, reduce me to nothing because that is the punishment I deserve. But he neither kills nor banishes me. He cannot even reject me. Instead he grasps hold of reality, twists it and turns it until it fits comfortably into his consciousness and tells me that physical fatherhood is irrelevant. There is, between him and this baby girl, a love so strong, so deep that it sweeps away such considerations. He is, of course, right. I agree with him. I want him to smash me over the head. I want him to shout, 'Bitch!' and 'Whore!' I have to be satisfied with rationality.

We begin a series of detailed and protracted analyses of my problems which have now, at long last, become his problems as well. We analyse my reasons for infidelity, my discovery that I really am a sexual person, my feeling that, for various deep and complicated reason, I find it difficult to express my sexuality with him. He comes up with the perfect solution. We should both, he feels, be free to indulge in extra-marital affairs. Such behaviour would not, he says, damage our marriage. On the contrary, it would remove the intensity of our battles and lead to greater harmony between us. We must not, however, run the risk of falling in love with other people. We must keep our activities purely on the level of sexual adventures.

What can I do but agree? It is the beginning of the end but I do not know that. Nor does he. It seems a reasonable and sensible thing to do. We grow. We change. We are not the children who married, vowing and believing in eternal love. I am aware of the fact that I will not abide by the terms of our agreement. I have, indeed, broken them already. I am in love with the Arab and love is against the rules.

Now he urges me on. He wants me to have an affair but I don't want to. I'm saving myself for the Arab's return. I am happy to live in the world of my fantasies. Every night my Arab lover comes to me and when my husband makes love to me I give to him the flooding overflow that belongs to another man. He thinks that my more passionate responses are the result of our enlightened sexual attitudes. He does not know that the only body I can enfold in my arms is that of the man ten thousand miles away.

Then the letter arrives that I have been waiting for. He is coming back, coming home to me. He loves me; he cannot live without me; I haunt his dreams. I am the source, the centre of all things to which he must return. My spirits soar. The year's separation has enabled me to see everything in perspective. I accept my marriage now and I accept the fact that it is also possible to love outside of the marriage. I don't have to make any choices. I don't have to give up either my marriage or my lover. I am a liberated woman indeed. I imagine again and again the moment of our reunion.

It is now almost the end of the teaching year and the long, summer holidays are about to begin. There is a man at work. We talk a lot and we have become friends. He attracts me and, I suppose, I attract him but we keep our relationship on a platonic, intellectual level. One day, as I am getting myself a cup of coffee in the staff room, he comes into the room. We are alone. On an impulse he kisses and all the feelings that we have confined beneath our conversations now come out and flow from lip to lip. 'I've been dying to do that all year,' he says and I'm surprised to find that I'm responding. I have no hesitation in arranging a meeting and I go to his flat the next day. It doesn't work sexually but it's warm and friendly and nice and it's just the sort of thing I can tell my husband about. By telling him this little, unimportant thing I can keep safe inside the secret of my real passion.

I tell him and he is delighted. Then I find out why. Now that I've confessed he can too and he tells me that he's been involved in an affair for months. His eagerness for me to have an affair now makes sense. He won't feel guilty about his affair if I'm involved in one too. My reaction is one of shock and anger and jealousy. My double standards astound me. I want to be free to carry on my extra-marital relationship but I don't want him to have the same freedom. I want him to want only me, to love only me, to be faithful to me.

We spend the holidays talking things out. His affair is threatening and frightening to me but we keep going over and over it and he reassures me that he loves me. I believe him because I need to believe him and because I see that he believes himself. I even take the children out one day a week so that he can have the house to himself to entertain his lady. He offers to do the same thing for me. Now I have the upper hand and I use my advantage to tell him that I will renew my relationship with the Arab when he returns. He doesn't seem to mind and when my lover arrives my husband gives me a free weekend to go away with the man I haven't seen for a year. What other husband, I tell myself, would allow his wife this measure of freedom.

It is strange to be with the Arab again, not at all like the imagined reunion. I feel nothing. No love, no hate, no passion, no despair. Nothing. What is wrong? Is it that the distance and the separation have lead me to idealise and exaggerate my feeling? Has fantasy won over reality? I don't know. I only know that the magic has gone. Or is it that he has finally and so totally capitulated to me, accepted the child as his own, realized that he is a slave to his love for me? Have I really just sought to make this man love me and now that I have won, now that he so openly loves me, do I just want to throw him away?

What terrible game do I now act out with this unfortunate man! I become the aggressor, the tormentor, the master – he becomes the victim, the submissive slave. I am merciless with him. My cruelty is compulsive. I deliberately hurt him, pick at him, fight him. What does he give me? He gives me a four volume edition of And Quiet Flows the Don, a record of Khachaturian dances, an antique clay vessel used by the Jews to collect their tears as they wept beside the wailing wall in Jerusalem, a handful of ancient coins, a wooden statue symbolizing love, a precious child. And what do I give him? Once I was Solomon's ring. Once I gave him all that any man could desire.

Now I shower him with the bitterness of my tongue, take out on him all the frustrations of my life. And he is helpless now and neither he nor I know why I am so terrible to him but we both accept the roles we seem compelled to play and wait for the drama to work its own way to the final tragic conclusion. And there is still the union, the passionate embrace – enemy to enemy.

Another year slides by. I let it, scarcely notice its passing. Thirty-six years old. Four children, aged two, four, six and eight. Mother, teacher, mistress, wife. A playwright without plays. Sometimes I scream at him, 'I'll never write while I'm married to you!' It's true. I know it. He knows it. Angry, embittered, frustrated, unfulfilled – I crash my way through the interminable, monotonous days – or eat my way through them.

I hate the long holidays. I'd much rather be at work. I don't like weekends and wish there were no end of term breaks. At work I can get outside of myself and my responsibilities. I love to teach and lose myself in the drama of the classroom. Home is full of undercurrents of our anger.

I look forward to the beginning of the teaching year. This year I am teaching English to migrants for the first time and I like the idea of a new challenge. Enrolment night is a nightmare with sixty or seventy New Australians doing tests, having them marked, being graded and placed in appropriate classes. There's one man I can't help noticing. He's in his forties, I suppose, warm, smiling, very attractive. When class begins the next night I'm delighted to see his face there. He's exuberant and outgoing, talkative and friendly. He comes from Hungary but he's been in Australia for quite a long time and speaks English well. There is, between us, an immediate attraction.

He flirts with me openly in the classroom and I respond openly. He asks me, in front of the whole class, if I will go and have dinner with him. I accept, openly, and afterwards we arrange a dinner date for the following week. I am behaving in a most unprofessional way but he almost dares me to and there is such good humour in his approach that I cannot resist responding.

He is, in many ways, every woman's dream. He is totally charming, disarming, self-confident. There is a twinkle in his eye and an assurance in his bearing that says he can have any woman he wants. I tell him that I have a husband and a lover. He says that doesn't bother him at all. He is in no hurry. He has infinite patience and time. He does not rush me, push me or make any sexual advances. He sits back, quite sure that I will come to him, waiting for me to make the first move. During dinner he tells me delightful and humorous stories of war experiences, smuggling, screwing in telephone booths. I feel that here is a man who has really lived a full and adventurous life. I've never been so genuinely delighted in a man's company. The gloomy husband and despairing lover shrink beside this handsome man who makes me laugh and laugh.

He still makes no move. He goes on being totally, effortlessly charming. I am very easily won. As we leave the restaurant and go to cross the road, it is I who take his hand. He responds with a pressure of warmth, but still takes no advantage of me. We sit in his car. Now it's his turn to move. He kisses me and I am surprised by the warmth and passion of his kiss. I can sense that he is a good lover and I tell him so. He, evidently, feels the same about me. But there is no hurry. We arrange a meeting during the day in a week's time.

I go home and my husband is awake, waiting for me, wanting to know what I've done. What was he like? How did I feel? Did I go to bed with him? I don't want to talk about it. I want to be left alone. He makes me tell him all about it. I have to go over every detail – the dinner, the kissing in the car, the plans for a further meeting. 'You're going to go to bed with him, aren't you!' he exclaims, his own excitement mounting. 'I know you are.'

'I'm not sure,' I reply, longing to be left alone.

'Tell me again how he kissed you,' he demands, starting to make love to me. What he's asking me to do makes me shudder with disgust. He doesn't worry about foreplay but starts to thrust himself into me. 'Talk about it!' he commands. 'Tell me what you feel when he kisses you.' My mouth wants to vomit but instead I let the words he wants to hear tumble out of my mouth until, with a final, hammering charge he comes inside of me and then it's over and I'm glad it's over and he lets me go and I am, for the briefest moment, free.

The week seems long to me. I want this new man and it feels good to be starting a new sexual adventure. When I get to his place and into his bed I can see at once that I'm in the hands of an expert. He is cool, careful, perfect. He brings me to powerful orgasm with calm precision. The he comes and, at that point, I am confronted by what I consider to be the eighth wonder of the world – his penis stays erect and it is to remain that way for the next two hours.

Afterwards we talk. He tells me that I have a very rare sexual capacity and that, of the thousands of women he's made love to, only one other woman exhibited the strength of orgasm that I seem to be capable of. He proceeds to give a careful, scientific analysis of our lovemaking, trying to teach me, in a technical way, to be aware of my vagina and its capacities. He intrigues me. I've never met a sex expert before. He has, he admits, devoted his entire life, from the time he turned eighteen to his present forty-four years to making love to women. I am, of course, delighted and flattered to find that I have such a capable cunt. He is the master, I the willing pupil. He lures me into a world where sex dominates, where orgasm is the prize, where all that is valued is the quality of the coming – an orgiastic banquet, a physical feast, where art of performance rather than emotion is the measure of success. Not with him the breathtaking hunger of the Arab, but rather the slow, deliberate excitation, the building climb to passion, the holding back, the going forward, the artistic weaving towards the unbelievable come.

He is a shift worker and I work odd hours. We can fit in many daytime meetings. I go to his place five days a week. I know I'm breaking the marriage rules but I don't care.

What is it that he is doing for me? It is not that he is making love to me but rather that he gives me free rein, allows me to examine and explore and extend my sexuality.

He is always in control, simply there – the ever erect penis on which I work my own way, in my own time, to my own end. His coming is immaterial to him and to me. He is just the vehicle for my self-discovery. I teach myself to attain the mysterious multiple orgasm. I stop only when my legs ache or my back aches – my cunt could go on forever. I am Woman – powerful, unleashed.

I give myself totally to this awakened sexuality without any regard to possible consequences. I am hooked, trapped, the willing victim of an insatiable lust. I am my cunt. Nothing else is.

My husband is furious. I have castrated him, reduced him to powerless frustration. He cannot compete. I throw in his face the fact that some other man is able to make me respond in this extraordinary way. It is intolerable to him to find that I have a sexuality that he could never unlock, a potential that he could never tap, a sexual expression that he will never witness. He feels bitter, rejected, jealous.

The Arab is furious, now almost at the point of breakdown. How can I, he wants to know, prefer sexual, animal gratification to what he has to offer? I thumb my nose at both of them. They can both get stuffed as far as I'm concerned. I've found Casanova and Rudolph Valentino all rolled into one and I'm not about to give him up – not for them and their reasonable, logical, biting, male intellects. I've had a belly-full of intellectuals! I'd throw them all away for the magic prick. How dare they throw reason at me! What have they got to offer? All they ever wanted, either of them, was to pull me down, destroy me, slice my brain into little pieces. I won't let either of them get into me.

I become, for a while, a kind of sexual football. I am thrown between the three of them, being screwed into a stupor. Sometimes I go to bed with all three of them on the same day. I do it deliberately – just to see if I can climax with each of them. If my husband thinks I've been with either of the others, then he wants me all the more. 'I don't care,' he says, 'I don't care who you screw as long as you save some for me!' And I don't care about anything at all any more. From morning till night my only thought is for the sexuality that has somehow taken over my being.

I want to be set free from the Arab and I use this new relationship to sever the old one. But the Arab becomes desperate and refuses to give me up. He demands access to the child. We do nothing but shout and scream at each other. He demands blood tests to prove that the child is his. He does not consider me fit to live, let alone being a suitable mother for his child. My husband, who has still never met the Arab, is furious with him for making such a fuss. Can't the man see that, by this stage, physical fatherhood is totally irrelevant? I agree with my husband but we all go to have blood tests. All three of us, I think, are a little afraid. It is a difficult time for each of us. I know, and have always known, what the blood tests will show. They will show, without doubt, that the child belongs to the Arab.

But I am wrong. I belong to one blood group. The Arab belongs to another. The baby and my husband have the same blood type, a third one that is different from either mine or the Arab's. Not only do they have identical blood groups, but both of their blood samples show an antipathy to the Arab's blood. She is my husband's child.

What terrible trick have I played on myself and on those around me? What pain have I caused all of us by my real feeling that I alone knew the truth? Did I just imagine his face in hers, in the swiftness of a movement, a gesture, a smile? It is difficult for me to accept that the wish for a certain thing to be true could so distort one's perception. And yet I have deceived myself.

The Arab is now in a corner. He is defeated, downtrodden, destroyed. The last trick he holds has failed him.

He demands to see me once more and promises that he will leave me alone after that. We meet. I am too afraid to go to his flat. We sit in the car and talk. He is so emotionally disturbed that he believes the blood tests prove him to be the father. He hears what he needs to hear, believes what he needs to believe.

We hurl abuse at each other. If we were not in the car, parked in a busy street, I think he we would kill each other. Raw venom spurts from our lips. He, whom I loved with such passion, I now hate with equal passion.

I watch him leave the car, slam the door, blinded by tears of outrage and despair, lost, shattered, destroyed. I watch him go and I know, with absolute clarity, that I have destroyed him. And he has let himself be destroyed by me. And isn't that, after all, the name of the game? In this relationship I have come out on top. I am the victor; my prize – the satisfaction of having reduced another member of the human race to a hollow, quivering shell.

I do not look upon myself with horror. I do not see what I have done as reprehensible. The victory gives me no lasting sense of power because the battle is over on only one front. I still have the marriage to crash and smash and batter my way through.

EIGHT

And what is he, this man with the magic phallus with whom I wallow and stuff and gorge my insatiable sexual gluttony? He is many things – professional gambler, smuggler, conman, thief. He entertains me constantly with stories that are full of excitement and danger and I experience, through him, what it is to be an adventurer in an unstable and unpredictable world.

I am lying beside him. He is quiet at the moment. I am lying close to him, his arms around me. 'Have you ever killed anyone?' I ask, softly. I hear the 'yes' from his heartbeat before I hear it from his lips.

Now I hear stories of a different kind – of murder and survival, of torture and imprisonment. He had been, he tells me, a smuggler with a difference. He had smuggled Jews out of Communist Hungary and brought medicines and drugs back into the country. All this was done for a very high price but within the boundaries of a strict, definitive, moral code. He and his friend had been captured and imprisoned and his friend had been executed. He tells me now of torture, of having all his toenails pulled out and his teeth smashed. I understand now why his mouth is a glittering mass of gold – a vain man's attempt to repair the damage wreaked on him by his guards.

And then he talks to me of revenge. Six guards, he tells me, inflicted torture upon him and after his release from prison he had sought out and killed five of them. The sixth came to Australia and he came here originally, he tells me, to track down and murder this man. I shiver beside him. Is he making all this up? I don't think so. I sense his inner violence and I know that he is telling me the truth. I am always attracted and lured and won by the violence in others. Perhaps I can sense that my own murderous instincts are safe if I allow myself to get lost in the destructive impulses of another.

And all this explains something else about him. His heart is ice. He never feels. He is a machine. 'Don't ever fall in love with me,' he warns. 'I'm not capable of loving.' I do not heed his warning. I let my emotions overflow and I set myself the task of breaking through his defences, of piercing his heart. I would like, just once, to see him weep and with his tears dissolve the barriers he puts between himself and me. His potential viciousness and the fact that he is a murderer challenge me to evoke a real emotional response. I find it very easy to commit myself to a man who might, at any moment, turn and smash me down.

The May holidays are nearly here and I suggest to my husband that we divide the vacation between us. I will take the children away to my sister's farm for the first week and then he can mind them while I go away for the second week. He agrees but, after the children and I have been at the farm for two days, he arrives to visit us and all I can feel is fury. Why has he turned up here, on his week off? Why does he pursue me? Why does he force me to have intercourse here, in my sister's house, on the lounge room floor? Why can't he feel my revulsion? Is he looking for rejection? Or is he here because he is a child who cannot stay alone at night in a dark and empty house? I despise him.

Now it is my turn to go away and I spend the week with my lover. Day after day of uninterrupted screwing. All this physical activity has kept me tiny and trim and I feel confident and secure. I ring my children every night to assure them and myself that everything is alright. I talk to my husband. He tells me about his lady. He is upset about her because her husband has attacked and bashed her. He suggests that, as I am not at home, she might move in for a few days if the situation with her husband becomes intolerable. I can, from my warm little love nest, afford to be magnanimous.

She is, he tells me, in any case, on the point of leaving her husband and is only prevented from doing so by the fact that she has very little money and would have to provide a home for herself and her two boys. Would I, he suggests, like to think about the possibility of her moving into our house for a few months, just on a trial basis. We are, after all, he says, mature people. It is obvious, he says, that I would like to be entirely free of the obligation of sleeping with him. Wouldn't we, he says, feel freer and better off if she were living with us. We believe, don't we, that the nuclear family is a suffocating and somewhat destructive unit. We feel, don't we, that extended family living would be preferable. We could, he claims, carry out a really modern and sophisticated living experiment. It would be better, wouldn't it, if the object of his sexual activities were in the house and easily accessible to him. That would mean, wouldn't it, that I would be free to visit my lover as often as I pleased without having to worry about leaving the children. And the children, of course, would not suffer at all. In fact they would know nothing about his relationship with the lady. They would just believe that we had chosen to extend our family to include another mother and two more boys. There would not, he assures me, ever be any public showing of affection between him and his lady. We would, to the rest of the world, simply be trying a new way of living to fit in with modern needs of working and raising children. He is very persuasive. It all seems perfectly reasonable to me. A little unusual and very daring, but quite reasonable. I tell him that I will think about his proposition very seriously and discuss it with him when I return. I talk it over with my lover. We examine the scheme, trying to find loopholes. There are none. We both see it as the mature solution to an eternal problem.

He brings her to meet me. I even like her. She is not at all like me. She is thin and blonde. At first this disappoints me, then it pleases me. We discuss our situation and decide to give it a go, agreeing that if any one of the three of us finds the situation too difficult to handle, we will immediately abandon the whole experiment. We are delighted with what we are about to do. We are like children who have just invented a new game.

I enter this living experiment with self-assurance and certainty. I have no hesitations, no doubts at all. And he is so anxious for it to work, so considerate, so eager to please me. Why shouldn't he be? Perhaps he sees himself as King of the Castle.

It doesn't take me long to realize that I don't like having six children in the house. Though none of the children are supposed to know about what is going on and though, on a conscious level, they probably don't know anything, the situation is tense and fired with explosive undercurrents. Five boys are too many, no matter whose they are. Sometimes I mind all six children, sometimes she does, sometimes my husband does. We all have our allotted times and our allotted household responsibilities.

What do I feel? Not what I expected. Things change. We all sit and talk at breakfast instead of him grunting over a newspaper and me eating while I feed the kids. We sit, she and I, drinking coffee at the same time. That means it's a social occasion. We have to communicate. I don't want to talk to her. Probably, she doesn't want to talk to me but we're obliged to. Maybe we are just getting to know each other. I end up talking too much, a habit I always slip into when I don't want to talk at all. I do it, I suppose, to fill in the spaces of the silence. We talk at breakfast, at dinner, while washing up the dishes. We are a friendly trio.

She doesn't eat much. I don't like that. She has just left her husband, moved into a strange house and, no doubt, the insecurity of her situation takes her appetite away. She only wants one slice of toast for breakfast. I want six. The less she eats, the more I eat. Within a week I am stuffing myself with food.

She disturbs me by the eagerness with which she rushes around clearing up after me. I always leave the coffee and the sugar out on the kitchen bench. She always puts them away. It doesn't look like home. He is pleased with the transformation. They both like the place to be much more orderly than I do. They are mother and father and I am the untidy child. They leave no space for me.

I buy new blankets for our double bed and start to cry as I put them on. 'Why are you crying?' he asks.

'Because the bed doesn't mean anything any more,' I reply.

'Aren't you coping?' he asks.

'Of course I am,' I reply, bursting into tears.

I go out a lot, not necessarily because I want to see my lover but because I don't want to stay at home. I often leave them alone in the house with the six children because I can't even feel that I belong there. She has, somehow, usurped me.

If I intend staying home, I go straight to my room after the children have gone to bed for the night. He doesn't want me to do that. He wants me to stay in the lounge room and take part in a cheerful, friendly, jolly conversation. I can't. I don't know why I can't. I go to my room. I try to read. They are still out in the lounge room. I want to go into the kitchen to make myself a cup of coffee or to get something to eat. I can't go out there because they are still out there. What are they doing? What are they talking about? I have to stay where I am. I don't dare to leave my room. I lie there, wondering what kind of things they say to each other. I am like a child shut out from its parents' room.

They leave the lounge room and I hear them go into her room. Her room is next to ours so that he can slip easily from room to room. Built-in cupboards divide the rooms. When he's in there with her I can hear their voices and I can hear their silences. When the silences become intolerable I jump out of bed and thump into the kitchen and eat all the chocolate biscuits and swallow two sleeping pills and clump back into my bedroom and stuff my ears with earplugs and lie rigid, waiting for sleep. He comes into our bed, hours later, and he curls up to me, expecting me to respond, wanting to make love to me. Sometimes I let him. I have come to hate the nights.

We have a big party at our house, full of students and teachers. My lover buys me an expensive, black, hand-embroidered, Rumanian dress. My husband is furious but I don't care and I flaunt my lover's generosity. He buys himself a black silk shirt for the occasion and he looks so suave and handsome.

At the party my lover ignores me. Why? He dances all night with a friend of mine who does not know that he and I are lovers. What is he trying to do to me? I watch him flirt with her. I tell myself that my lover can't spend all evening with me. If he did, then everyone would know that we were lovers and, as I'm still married, I should keep my affair secret. But I notice that my husband has no such sense of propriety and he's deliberately staying with his lady all night. I am mortified and would like the floor to open and swallow me up. The only way I can handle the situation is by drinking too much. I feel myself reeling and I go to bed and pass out. The party ends without me.

I know my lover is having an affair with my friend. I sense it. I ask him outright and he denies it, but I know he's lying. I want to ask her but I can't. She's married. We are friends but not intimate friends. She wouldn't ask me whether I was faithful to my husband or not and so I can't ask her. One day I see her driving along in her car. She has a dreamy, wanton, sexual look on her face. I know she is going to him. An hour later I drive past his flat and I see her car parked outside. An empty terror opens up inside of me.

I see him that night. I am full of venom, anguish, complaint, hostility, criticism. Why did he lie to me? How could he do this to me? His face is impassive, the cold veneer I can never penetrate. No feelings there. No sense of loyalty. Concerned only for himself – cool and calm. Had he ever, he wants to know, said he loved me? Had we ever agreed upon fidelity? He was my friend, my lover, always available when I needed him, his door always open, his cock always ready. What more did I expect?

What do I want? What do I expect? 'Love,' I want to cry, 'Love! Love! Love!'

He can, after all, manage two women at once. He has never, in twenty-five years of sexual activity, been found wanting. He is quite able to handle two or three or four relationships at the same time. Sex is, after all, his talent. Why am I being so infantile? Why am I being so unreasonable?

I have to accept. There is no alternative. He asks me for my key back. He needs, now, to know what times I will be coming to visit him. I ask him, dreading the answer, whether he has given her a key. He has! My stomach sinks. Why? I insist on knowing why. Because, he tells me, a completely unexpected thing has happened to him – he has actually fallen in love with her. He still wants me to be his mistress but he loves her. I am jealous, furious, full of hatred and despair but I have to accept his terms. I am a slave to the sexuality that he has awakened in me and I am appalled by the fact that I do not have sufficient dignity to get up and walk away.

Now I become desperate. There is nowhere to turn. I am second best with my lover, second best with my husband. I must have someone with whom I can be first – or I'll sink and die. I am breaking down but no one seems to notice.

One night, I go out into the kitchen unexpectedly and I see the two of them – my husband and his woman. They are in the lounge room. He has his arm around her. He moves away as soon as he sees me but it's too late. What will I do when I run out of sleeping pills? Another night, he is in her room and it's very late and I can't get to sleep and I am compelled to get up and bash on their door and I make him come out. 'How long are you going to be in there?' I cry.

'We're just doing the crossword,' he replies and I go back to bed and block my ears but even then I imagine that I can hear their bed springs and I wonder what I will do if any of the children should come upstairs during the night. I live in terror of the sounds that are made by the other people who inhabit my house. They have infiltrated every crevice. They have bitten into my brain. There is nowhere left for me at all.

He, the tom-cat, purring from room to room. She, the good mother, cooking, cleaning – busy, busy, busy. Me, the baby, random and diffuse – orgiastic ingestion of chocolate biscuits and penises.

But in the classroom I exhibit an absolute mastery and ability. I have never taught so well. My intellect works with superb efficiency. I hold on to my teaching as if it is the only area in my life in which I can manipulate, command and control myself. In the classroom, then, I project my power.

In the bed I am still mistress of the mighty orgasm but my lover and I have been reduced to cunt and cock and when I leave him I must stuff myself with food, eating him up because he does not love me and because I need to fill my insides as a safeguard, a measure of protection against a hostile world.

When I walk into my house I am blanketed in despair. I have become a baby, longing and needing to be cradled and held. There are no protecting arms to hold me soft, warm, secure. And my children's love will not do because I am a child and can no longer function as a mother. I reject them all and, at the same time, feel guilty for rejecting them. Does my oldest son suspect? Does he have fantasies about me and other men? Where does he think I go to when I leave the house at night? Why don't I think of him, of them, of these precious children of mine? What damage am I doing them?

I start to realize that it's hopeless and that, if I am to survive, then she, the usurper, must go. Yet I feel afraid of my decision. I am afraid that he, my husband, will punish me for hurting her.

I look at myself and I look at my children. I now understand. All that has happened I have allowed to happen. Does my seeing entitle me to forgiveness?

I circle my children, wings swooping down, warm and protecting around them. I don't know what he will do when I tell him she has to go. I cling to my children. Can they and I, if necessary, go on alone? She has to go. I can see that she has to go. But I'm terrified of him. What will he do to me when I tell him she has to go?

The thing I fear most is that he will try to talk me into letting her stay so I go about removing her in the only way I can. I leave home and I go to stay at my lover's flat. Then I ring up my husband and I tell him that she has to go and that I will not return home until she and her children are gone, gone, gone.

And while I am staying at my lover's place I dream a dream that sets me free. I am sleeping on his lounge. I think I'm awake and I think I can hear a mouse, then I think it's a rat and finally I'm convinced it's a bigger animal. I can feel it, crawling on my arm, pinning me helpless on the lounge. I look up and see three more animals poised above me, ready to drop down and devour me. The animal's face is close to mine. I can see its large teeth, feel its hot breath. I try to call to my lover for help but the sounds are muffled in my throat. I am determined to set myself free. I struggle and fight and, with enormous effort, I suddenly feel that I'm able to move my arm. As soon as my arm moves, the animal's face becomes a cardboard caricature and, at that moment, I realize that I am dreaming. The beast is my husband, but he has a cardboard face. I have no need to be afraid of him – not now.

It is marvellous, then, to come home, to breathe the air, to feel it's mine, to hug my children, to beg their forgiveness. I want to start again and I promise myself that I will be a good and loving mother from now on.

It is a biting, tearing time that has to be battled through before we can end our marriage. He cannot decide whether or not to leave me. He hates me for sending her away; he hates me for putting him into a situation that might force him to leave his children. Especially, he is reluctant to leave them in my care for he hates me now with such deep bitterness that he sees me as an ineffectual and unsuitable parent.

I hate him, with a dull, cold hate. I dream that my husband is an old man and that he is trying to make love to me. He revolts and disgusts me. I go to the bathroom and find that my towel is covered with shit and blood. No new white towels for me. My husband has befouled my house with excrement.

Often he stays out all night and I fight with him because I think the children will find his behaviour strange and disturbing. He doesn't care. I have begun to see what we are doing to our children. He can only see what I have done to him.

I move into the bedroom that she has vacated. I will no longer share a room with him. I buy myself a new purple blanket. I will be Queen, if only of my own domain.

I dream of my lover. His face is the handle of a magic wand. His eyes can mesmerize and hypnotise me. It seems that, for me, the power of the penis is to win and sway me to submission. I keep going back to him, to experience again and again the magic of the golden prick.

My husband still will not decide whether to leave us or not. We continue to snap and snarl and bite and devour each other. We cannot stop fighting. It is very disturbing. I am filled with depression and despair.

One night, I go to visit my lover. He is expecting me. His car is in the carport. His lights are on. I knock on the door but he does not answer. I knock again. I go away and telephone him. He does not answer the phone. I keep ringing, every five minutes. He doesn't answer.

I am glad to find that I have sufficient self-respect to realize that I cannot allow myself to be humiliated in this way. I ring him the next day in a state of fury, abuse him and end the relationship. He remains calm, smiling into the phone. The breaking up of my marriage has so disturbed me that he can no longer put up with me and so he has engineered a humiliation so great that he knows I will end the affair. He gives me some good advice, as a parting gesture. 'Next time you get involved in a relationship,' he says, 'make sure that you are the one who dominates.'

So now I am left without a penis and, for me, that is an intolerable situation to be in. I have, for the whole of my sexual life, been dependent on men for my satisfaction. I have never been able to masturbate to orgasm and, although I try, I fail and I'm left in a fury of sexual frustration.

And I crumble and dissolve because I have no man. I try to win my husband back. I grovel at his feet, begging for love. And he delights in his revenge, paying me back for all the times he's wanted me and I've refused him. I weep. I beg. I plead. I long to start again. I tell him I'll be a good girl, a good wife, a good mother. He mocks me, rejects me, hates me. I scream and bash my head against the cupboard door and fall, stunned, to the floor. He stands above me and looks at me with disdain. 'And that,' he says, 'is what I am supposed to leave in charge of my children.'

We break the pattern of our mutual destruction by my going away for a ten-day boat trip. He tells me he will decide what he will do while I am away. I get onto the boat a cringing, snivelling mess but, as I move further and further away from home, I am able to see our situation more objectively and I know that he will leave me. I also know that I will manage.

I come back healthy and strong and black from the sun. He wants to make love to me and he chases me round the house all day. When the kids finally go to bed we make love swiftly, passionately, satisfyingly and, for the briefest moment, he allows me to believe that everything will be alright. And then he looks at me. 'Now,' he says, 'I'll tell you what I've decided to do. I'm going to leave you.' Warm tears slide down my cheeks. It is all over. He leaves on Christmas Day, four days after our thirteenth wedding anniversary.

And from the moment he leaves I feel a sense of relief and I know quite well that I am ready, at last, to walk alone. I move around in my London bed. I feel my arms and my legs. I look outside and see that night has fallen. Time to get dressed, to go out and eat, to enjoy a last evening at a London theatre. I think of my children, so far away, and I am flooded with their warmth and their love. They are always with me. Husbandless I may be but I am not alone.

NINE

I am reluctant to leave the London I have come to love yet eager for a new experience. Paris! How excited we are, my friend and her son and I, at the prospect of a week in Paris. We arrive in Paris at night with nowhere to stay and we are very proud of our ability to get ourselves to the Latin Quarter by Metro and find ourselves a very cheap hotel.

I think of Paris as the city of gaiety and romance, a magic wonderland where couples walk, hand in hand, down the Champs-Elysees. Surely, in Paris, I will suddenly and miraculously meet my Knight in Shining Armour, the charming, handsome Frenchman who will sweep me off my feet.

It is January. It is cold in Paris – cold and bleak and wet. The rain is relentless, the wind biting, the people hostile. I have a smattering of school-girl French but my halting attempts to speak are met with impatience by the people of Paris. After the first few rude rebuffs I'd rather get lost than ask anyone the way. I wash all my clothes by hand rather than face the prospect of a French laundromat. Foreign currency bewilders me and prices seem terribly high. My friend and her son have different interests to me and we tend to go our own separate ways although we meet for dinner together at night.

It is my first experience of being in a non-English-speaking country and I am afraid. Every time I cross a road I feel that the motorists would take a great delight in ploughing me down. I am frightened to walk in the streets at night and I see everyone as a potential enemy. I feel altogether alien. I cannot read a newspaper or watch television or go to a film or see a play. My hopelessness with the language labels me as an imbecile.

My fear drives me inside. I haunt museums and art galleries and spend my days absorbing the art treasures of Paris. Here I feel safe, still and quiet, locked into the creative visions of others.

After six days in Paris, it is time for my friend to leave. I wish I were leaving with her but my train tickets to Greece were purchased in London and the red tape involved in changing the bookings is too confusing to be contemplated. I have to remain in Paris for twenty-four hours on my own. So we decide to celebrate our last night in Paris together by going to a restaurant called The Balkans.

The restaurant is very crowded and we cannot find a table to ourselves. Each table is designed to seat six people so we join one that is already occupied by two Frenchmen. They speak in French and we speak in English. They eat their meal and we eat ours. We ignore each other and yet we are aware of each other. I try to decide whether or not to have any coffee because it's so expensive. Suddenly the man next to me tells the waiter to bring me coffee and indicates that he will pay for it and then starts to talk to me in halting English. He tells me that he would like to practise his English for a while if I don't mind. This is the first time that anyone in Paris has spoken to me and I take his approach as a simple gesture of friendliness. We begin to have a conversation. He looks about sixty years old and I find out that he is cultured and well-educated. He has a PHD in Physics, works in research and tutors, part-time, at the Sorbonne. He knows every art gallery in Paris and I enjoy talking to him even though his English is so poor.

He wants me to go for a walk with him. I see no reason to be afraid of him and I agree to go. We walk down the street and I am delighted that a charming old Frenchman is going to show me something of the sights of Paris. Within one minute

I realize that I've made a mistake. He wants me to go to bed with him. I feel disappointed because I would really like to just talk to him, to get to know him. I try to explain this to him. Absurdly, I go so far as to say that I don't want to absorb penises, I want to absorb the world. Of course, he has no idea what I am talking about.

He takes me to a café and we sit and drink wine and talk. I enjoy learning about him. He lives in Paris and he tells me that he has never married because he has always been too selfish to accept the responsibilities of marriage. He is the eternal student, so involved in his own studies that this has become his life. He is very small, thin and frail. His hair is thinning, his beard neat, pointed, grey.

I tell him that I, also, prefer to live without a mate because I need to write. We develop a wary appreciation of each other but I can see that he is determined to break down my resistance and he keeps returning to the subject of sex. He seems puzzled. He struggles for the English words to ask me whether I am, perhaps, either frigid or a lesbian. Paris is, after all, the city of romance and I am a woman alone in Paris. I reject him, quite firmly, and ask him to show me the way back to my hotel. He smiles, lifts his hands in a gesture of defeat, and asks me to have dinner with him the next night. I agree on the condition that sex is not mentioned.

The next night I go downstairs to meet him at the appointed time outside my hotel. It is very cold on the street and I wait for ten minutes but the Frenchman doesn't appear so I go back up to my room. I read a book for an hour and then decide that I'm starving. It's 9pm and I'll have to find the courage to go out and eat alone.

I leave my hotel and there he is, waiting for me. His presence is unexpected. I have already decided that he has stood me up. But there he is, smiling, bowing, apologizing – sorry he's late, held up at the Sorbonne, couldn't get away, has just booked himself into my hotel, isn't that convenient? I am shocked. He has actually taken a room at my hotel so that he can be near me. I am insulted and flattered at the same time. I don't know what to do about him.

We go to dinner and we eat and drink and talk and I can tell that I am going to go to bed with him after all. Not, I tell myself, because he's taken me out for dinner, not because he wants me enough to have moved into my hotel, but because I want to, because he's charming and clever and, to be honest, out of a feeling of curiosity. I've never made love to anyone as old as he is and a part of me wants to know what it might be like. From this point of view he both attracts and repels me.

Throughout dinner he tries to persuade me to stay in Paris for another week. His seduction technique is so obvious that it is laughable and I find it all the more amusing since it is unnecessary. After all, I've already decided that I will go to bed with him but I keep this decision to myself.

We walk back to the hotel and he is quite surprised when I tell him that I will go with him to his room. We enter the room and get undressed and again I feel this mixture of attraction and repulsion. He is spidery thin and his hands are gnarled and the skin creases into deep wrinkles on his neck. His shoulders are rounded and his chest caves in a little. The skin on his arms is dry and his pubic hair is sparse and grey. But the skin around his penis is milk white and I see fine blue veins tracing their way across the transparent softness of his groin. I want to touch him but at the same time I don't want to look at him. So I turn out the light.

The little room is dark. His kisses are soft, sensuous, his tongue gentle and lingering. He is the kind of lover for whom caressing, kissing, arousal are more important than orgasm. I like that kind of lover. His joy is in the waiting. He moves me on top of him. He is so fragile that I feel frightened I might crush him, smother him. But his hands are firm and his penis hard and strong. I lose my fear. I put my hands behind his head and feel again a moment of distaste. His hair is so thin, so dry, his scalp soft and vulnerable. I move very gently and I feel his pleasure in the way I move. He is almost passive beneath me. I would like to be slow, I would like to wait, I would like to take my time but I am excited by his stillness and I reach orgasm very quickly. He pulls me down beside him and turns me on my side. We lie with our stomachs and thighs touching, his penis inside me. He becomes faceless, ageless. He is any man and every man as he guides me on a gentle, loving ride through the dark Paris night.

When it is over he turns to me and says, 'Now, you will stay.'

'No,' I reply. 'I will not stay.' He cannot believe that I do not want to stay. He is offended and suggests that we go to sleep. I will surely change my mind in the morning.

'I prefer to sleep alone,' I say and get out of bed and put on my clothes.

Then he tells me that he will find some way to make me stay in Paris. Suddenly I am afraid. Can a charming sixty-year-old Frenchman with a PhD find some way to prevent my leaving Paris? I really don't know. Has he a source of hidden strength that will enable him to hit me over the head and steal my passport and keep me here against my will?

My fear is very real as I leave the room and agree to meet him the next morning at breakfast. I am relieved by the fact that he does not get up to stop my going.

I know I won't be able to sleep so I go downstairs to the small hotel lounge room and buy myself a jug of hot milk coffee and curl up in a comfortable chair and sip my coffee and, after a few minutes, I start to feel quite pleased with myself. I have, after all, stood up for myself. I think about the French-man upstairs and I decide that he can't really do anything to harm me. I convince myself that I'm just as strong as he is, physically, and that all I need do is to avoid him until I leave Paris. I now start to feel warmed by my self-sufficiency. It is good to be alone.

And with that thought, my mind goes back to the marriage break-up, three years ago, and to the initial bitterness of having been left alone. It seems to me, as I walk down the street, that there is always an empty space beside me. I look at other people holding hands and there is no hand to hold mine. When I wake up in the morning a sudden panic fills me as if I have forgotten during the night and then come each day to face anew the shock of having to go on alone. I am a separated wife. He lives with his lady; he has someone to love. I live alone; I have no one to love. I hate him and I hate her and feel an overriding sense of the unfairness of it all.

There are, though, many things that I like about being alone. Each night, as I stretch out in my big double-bed, I delight in the luxury of sleeping alone. And I feel, on the whole, that a great, gloomy cloud has gone from my house for he was, indeed, a very sullen and cranky man. The children and I feel a lightening of spirits in the knowledge that he is no longer here to criticise us and tell us what to do. We do, of course, over-react to a certain extent. We never put our clothes away, never close any cupboard doors, allow books, papers and possessions to pile up on the dining room table, and still have Christmas wrappings on the floor at the end of January. The whole house becomes a play area – they even leave toys in the toilet. We walk about, all five of us, making as much mess as we please. There is no critical father to tell us to put our things away.

They develop an almost immediate resentment against their father. They depend much more on me. They make, all four of them, the choice that must be made and, without consciously realizing it, they give their total allegiance to me. He doesn't see this. He believes that by having them stay two nights week with him he will retain some say in what they are and what they will become. He is wrong. I know that, straight away. From the moment he leaves I understand that I, alone, am responsible for my children.

The children believe that their love is enough for me. It is not enough but I don't want them to know that I need anything more than their warm and generous caresses. I don't want them to know that I need men and I keep my sexual life separate from them. I feel a kind of terror now that I am cut off from any regular and dependable source of sexual satisfaction and my sexual drive increases because I know that I have no predictable outlet. I start to pick up men indiscriminately. I don't care who or what they are. All I need is a stiff prick for a few minutes and I can climax. In the first three weeks after the marriage break-up I have intercourse with nine different men. My upbringing should make me disgusted with my behaviour but I am not. My promiscuity gives me the confidence that I can find as many sexual partners as I need. I think I'm making very good use of the two nights a week that I am free of my children.

And then, in the middle of January, I am invited to a party given by one of my ex-students. I hate going to parties but I force myself to go and it proves to be a very eventful night for me.

I am introduced to a man who writes plays. He is sitting on the stairs, removed and unsociable, - a strange looking man, dark-skinned, teeth missing, magnetic eyes and, incongruously, a broad Australian drawl. He has had a play read by the group who produced my play and we talk a little about writing but he is strangely ill at ease. He keeps looking around him, seems disturbed. When I tell him that I have not been able to write for years he tells me that he has a way of breaking through creative blocks that might help me. He tells me that he will do my astrological chart and talk to me about creativity if I'd care to come and visit him. He gives me his address, carefully written on a piece of paper. He is not making a pass at me. I'm sure of that. He intrigues me and I'd like to keep talking to him but he gets up and abruptly leaves the party without saying goodbye to anyone. I feel disappointed.

I go to the kitchen to get a glass of wine. How I hate parties! How shy I am, how socially inept. I can smile and talk but I don't really want to. For me it is all an enormous strain. I want to sit down and cry because I married the wrong man for the wrong reasons and I don't want to be standing here making social chit-chat. I want to be married to the right man for the right reasons.

A man comes up to me and starts to talk to me. He works at Channel 2. He works in graphics and he's making a film. He is very quiet and unassuming. He tells me that he lives next door.

He takes my hand and asks me if I will go home with him. Why not? Another man, another room, another bed. I don't give a damn about any of them.

I go with him. His bed is a mattress on the floor and it has orange and black sheets. He lights incense sticks and puts on a weird record called 'Phaedra'. He plays it over and over again as he makes love to me. He takes me. I don't respond. He calls me 'innocent'. This offends me and I begin to make love to him with all the expertise I've learned from my professional lover. I feel his amazement as I skillfully climax again and again. I'll show him innocence! The sheets are drenched with my coming and I feel the self-satisfaction of showing him that I really do know how to screw. Does he think I come like that just for him? I can come like that with any man, any man at all – giving nothing but my cunt, keeping the whole of myself withdrawn.

He lies beside me, gentle, calm. He is forty-two years old but he doesn't look it. He is thin and his chest sounds weak. His bones are small and his frame fragile. He clings onto me as if he hasn't held a woman for a long time. He looks at me in the dim light. 'You're a real Earth Mother,' he says, softly.

His words move me. He has stripped me, uncovered my essence. For I am, indeed, an Earth Mother, wide and generous, flowing and fathomless. I have not tricked him for one moment. And because he has seen beneath my sexual mask, a flood response is released in me and I feel love flow up my thighs, across my belly, down my arms to my very finger tips and he and I make love again and this time I give him, not just my cunt, but the whole of my being.

It is almost morning and I tell him that I must go. He holds onto me, clings to me, doesn't want me to leave. He holds me as if this is the last time he will ever make love. We make love again with the total harmony of giving. It is 5 am. I really feel I must go. He still holds onto me, telling me that I am like a harbour where he can, for a moment, feel safe and secure.

Fool that I am! Stupid, idiotic fool! I think that this night is the beginning of something beautiful. I actually ask him when I will see him again. Then he tells me that it can only be this one night. He is free in spirit and does not involve himself in relationships. He would prefer to go without sex for a whole year and then have one perfect night like this. We could never, he assures me, repeat the beauty of this night. I want to burst into tears like a child. I feel cheated and deprived. How can he mean what he is saying? But he does mean it. I feel that I have given myself for nothing.

I decide to go and see the strange man I met at the party. There is a constant need to fill in the times when the children are not with me. I am afraid to be alone with myself and I would like to find some magical solution to my problem of being unable to write. I think he might have a cure. I am always looking to others to find a formula that might work for me. I would prefer to grasp onto someone else's way rather than make the effort of finding my own.

What is he, this man who I hope might turn out to be a prophet? I find him an intriguing and highly individualistic man. He is Anglo-Indian. He was an accountant, then did a university degree in English and Philosophy and is now a writer, part-time astrologer, part-time taxi driver who lives on the dole. He has rejected the conventional need for money and material possessions. He has carved out for himself the freedoms of time and space. I envy and admire him.

There is, between us, an immediate and powerful response. I don't believe in astrology but when he talks to me about it I am convinced that there must be some substance to what he is saying. He has entered his study of astrology as a sceptic, undertaken it to disprove it, and finds that he believes in it. Within a few hours he sways my mind. Does he really convince me or is it just that I am so ready to be intellectually won by yet another man's vision? He does my chart and is able to tell me extraordinary truths about myself. Middle decant Leo, Capricorn rising, Moon in Libra, Mercury in Virgo. As he explains the meaning of each of these I see myself slot into the interpretations that he gives. How does he do it? Is he just highly intuitive, tuned in to the subconscious minds of others? He certainly believes that what he does is based on a scientific study of the subject and, at first, that is what I accept.

Our lesson then gets on to the thing I've been waiting for. He tells me how to get rid of a writing block. His answer to this problem lies in the use of drugs. I try not to show how shocked I am. Marihuana and I have never met, never even come into close proximity before. He teaches me about drugs. He does not take drugs in order to have a good time but because of what they can teach him and because they enable him to write from different levels of perception. He is a high priest of LSD trying to woo and win me to its value as a key to the opening up of new mind experiences. I listen to him, breathless. It's like watching the first men land on the moon. He takes me and leads me by word and description into a world that sounds like a mixture of Paradise and Hell. It annoys me that I cannot comment. I can neither agree with nor refute what he is saying because I am outside his experience. It's like being a virgin when everyone around you is talking about sex.

He teaches me on another level. He introduces me to headphones and rock music. I listen to the Moody Blues, the Beach

Boys, Eno and Brian Ferry. He forces me to listen in such a way that I will realize that these musicians have discovered new levels of perception that the straight world refuses to recognize. He relates this music to the world of drugs, bombarding me with so many new ideas that my head reels.

I am afraid of drugs but his intellect, his promises, his reassurances, his charisma win me. I smoke marihuana with him and I like the feeling it gives me – the colours of the room, the way the musical instruments separate and individualise themselves. I feel comfortable with him. I am really surprised when he starts to seduce me because I have not been thinking of him in sexual terms but I feel so mentally stimulated by him that I am pleased to go to bed with him. I sense that my sexuality is too strong for him. He tells me that is because he is an Earth person and I am a Fire person. Is he right, or is this just his method of explaining away his own sexual inadequacies? He tells me that he only ever wants to make love to a woman once and then he likes to get onto the more important aspects of establishing a relationship. But I'm not going to let him leave me frustrated and I insist on making love a second time. I suspect that my climax terrifies him and I don't know whether to be flattered or insulted when he tells me that hasn't even read about my kind of orgasm. He makes me feel like a freak. He tells me that I ought to curb my sexuality and channel it into my writing. I tell him that he is wrong and that it is essential to express one's sexual drive in a physical way.

He and I develop what is to me a strange relationship. It is not normal because there is no sex in it. I always want to make love to him and he always wants to listen to music and to talk. There is no compromise. He never gives in. I go to him usually in a state of sexual frustration and our conversations became an arena where both intellect and sexuality meet, combat, come together, separate. It is a sexual affair of the spirit and of the mind. At the end of a four or five hour session with him I am no longer sexually frustrated and I am intellectually satisfied. Because it is not a sexual affair I need to satisfy my sexuality elsewhere. This infuriates him. He behaves as if I have been unfaithful to him.

One night I go to visit an Italian friend of mine. He is always ready to make love to me, casually, if that is what I want. If he is not busy and I am not busy we might decide to satisfy each other's sexuality. A no-strings-attached, friendly relationship. He always cooks me spaghetti and gives me fine wine to drink and plays soft, romantic music. He has a friend with him on this particular night – a tall, dark, handsome Yugoslav-Italian. At first I do not see what the game is and then I understand it. He means this night to end up with the three of us in bed. The idea repels me, then it excites me. Why not? This is something that is forbidden, naughty, just not done. For these reasons the idea attract me. My sexuality is a kind of badge at the moment. I want to outdo any man I end up in bed with. I want to prove that I have a stronger sexual drive than he does. This is a real challenge. They both make love to me, sometimes both together, sometimes one at a time. I am insatiable. There are hands and mouths and pricks and balls all over the place. It seems as if there are ten men in bed with me instead of two. I cannot climax properly and keep coming in short, inadequate orgasms that only make me more frustrated.

I go home feeling pretty smug. Look at me, living out what others only dare to dream about! I go to sleep exhausted and then I dream the dream of the tribunal.

In my dream the dawn light exposes me to a stern tribunal of steel-grey matrons, upright and rigid in their high-backed chairs. I don't know why I have been summoned before them. Why call me here? What have I done that I must be judged by the mothers of the world?

I stand before them – vulnerable. They don't speak. Their silence eats into me and I start to feel uncomfortable. 'What do you want from me?' I ask. My question vibrates across the stillness of their silence. The voiceless answer of their judgment communicates itself to me. Don't they bend at all, these women? And how do they arrive at their rigidity? Is there a turning point, a magic moment in time, when one ceases to be a child and becomes an awesome mother? Will it happen to me? Will I become one of them some day? They terrify me. They make me want to run and hide. They are all my mother and they all hurl her judgment at me. Mothers of children do not behave as I have behaved. Mothers are responsible people – not instinctual, irresponsible, animalistic individuals who hop into bed with two men at a time! Their eyes accuse me, condemn me as unfit for my role. I want to tell them that I'm a hurt and lonely child. I look for the words to defend myself but I can't find them and my mute defence flies back at me, unaccepted.

I turn from them, ashamed. Of course, they are right. I am irresponsible, unfit for motherhood. I leave the court of judgment, accepting my guilt and I zigzag through the high-walled alleyways of my mind and at each turn I manage to lose myself deeper and deeper in the unravelled tangle of my brain. I wander along, lost and alone.

I grow very tired in my wanderings and I am ready to sit down and cry out my despair when suddenly I hear the echoing of running footsteps and the sound of a heart pounding with such force that I almost feel as if it is beating inside of me. I turn and see before me the frightened face of my oldest son. I look at him and he looks at me and, deep inside my womb, I feel the powerful pull of the link that enabled him to find his way to me. Our child eyes meet and exchange a glance of mutual understanding and I put my arm around his shoulders and we turn and walk for a long, long time and, somehow, we manage to find out way home.

I wake up full of self-loathing vowing to be a better mother, to give up sex, to write a play, to manage, to make something of myself, to clean up the house. My resolutions have no substance. I continue to float in others.

He's pushing me to take LSD. If only he'd woo me sexually the way he woos me with drugs. LSD is his lady, his goddess, his Muse. He wants me to make her mine.

He tries to solve the problem of my sexuality. He invites another playwright over for me to meet. The three of us sit and talk and drink wine. Suddenly he says, 'Why don't you two go upstairs and screw while I cook dinner.' I let him manipulate me. I do what he suggests. I don't assert what is right for me. I don't even know what is right for me. I just let happen to me what he thinks is right for me. Afterwards he comes into the room and cuddles me and I can feel that his penis is hard next to me and I start to cry because I feel so confused and I don't really understand what he is doing to me. He both rejects me and holds onto me: his mind and his spirit are bound to me while his body rejects me. I am struggling with the lesson that he wants me to learn, that I must channel this random, childish sexuality of mine into proper creative channels.

And I begin to understand what he means, for I start to write for the first time in thirteen years. Poetry starts to flow out of me. It is emotional, bitter, hard and inferior poetry but it is writing none the less. Every day a poem forms in my brain and every night I write it down. I am creating at last.

I try to follow his precepts, to do things his way but I constantly fail. My cunt twitches and aches. I cannot tolerate my sexual frustration. I still can't masturbate to orgasm so I'm still driven to seek out men though, now, each encounter fills me with self-disgust.

A man picks me up at the beach. He is a Mr Universe type. He pounds my cunt until it swells with bruises and cuts. I can barely walk for a week.

My Italian friend takes me to meet a friend of his whose wife has left him. The abandoned husband cooks us a marvellous spaghetti and we eat and drink wine. Then my Italian friend says he'll wait in the lounge room while I make love to his friend. I don't walk out. I have no respect at all for myself or for my body. Perhaps I want to be a slut, a whore. Perhaps I even enjoy the shame and despair that they inflict on me. Perhaps it is simply that such times of adjustment are always difficult. I don't know. All I know is that I try to be satisfied with just an intellectual relationship but I'm not satisfied with it at all.

I agree to take a trip on LSD. I approach it with a mixture of excitement and apprehension. I don't really want to do it. I'm doing it because he wants me to do it. He has it all planned. We go to Circular Quay and drop the acid about fifteen minutes before getting on a Manly ferry. About half way there I start to feel that I am God. There's a tightening sensation in my forehead and I feel very tall and excitement bubbles through me. I want to laugh but he won't let me. This is a lesson and he makes me look closely at the waves until I can discern all the individual movements and patterns of the current. I can look and see and understand the structure of the sea. Then he directs my attention to the clouds. I realize that I have never seen the sky like this before. The clouds don't just move in one direction. I can see a multiplicity of movements within each cloud and the part each plays in the total movement of the clouds across the sky. I do not believe that the drug is altering my perceptions but that it enables me to see the true structure of natural phenomena. He tells me, and I believe, that LSD makes the essential nature of things observable. As we get off the ferry and start to walk through Manly and up on to an isolated hill behind the beach I become aware that I am now able to see the real nature of the people we pass. One man looks at me in a slightly sexual way and I see his face as an enormous, distorted leer. I pass a teenage girl and see, beneath her face, unhappiness and pain.

We reach the top of the isolated hill behind the beach and he puts on the tape recorder he has brought with him and plays the music of the Moody Blues. I look about me, at the swinging panorama of the sky and as the music cries out to me he teaches me that what the music is saying and what I am seeing are one and I know that he is right and, with wonder and awe, I look about me and know that I have found Paradise.

He turns off the music. I want it to go on, to be lost in it and in the sky about me. I long to fly into the cosmos, to be it, to know it, to feel it. He will not let me. My lesson has only just begun. Now he lectures me on the nature of the oneness of all things, of the earth and the sun and the moon and the planets. Do I feel the universal flow of Nature? Do I feel my oneness with existence? Indeed, I do. We sit down, side by side, and I hold his hand and close my eyes. He is angry with me and tells me to open my eyes. I must look and see. But I refuse and tell him that I want to take my own trip and that what goes on in my brain when my eyes are closed is too marvellous to miss. And so he gives in and he joins me on my trip. We sit very close and we concentrate very hard and we try to come onto the same level as each other. And we do it. We actually do it! We see the same visions, experience the same feeling, flow together on the same level of creation. He flows into me and I flow into him and we both flow into the universe. He is one with me and I am one with him and we are one with all that is. I know that what I am feeling now I have felt once before but have forgotten. I felt it in the womb, in the flowing oneness with my mother, as I lay cradled warm in her swaying fluid. I feel it now, here with him.

I know that he and I are feeling the same thing and taking the same trip and I know that this is quite an extraordinary thing for two people to be able to do and I wonder to myself if he will later deny the fusion of our union.

The sun starts to set and he is no longer joined to me. He is shivering with cold and he is afraid. I'm burning with heat. I am the sun and I'm not afraid. He tells me that it's time to come down but I refuse – I'm high, on fire. The birds, he tells me, are starting to twitter in the sky. It is time for all creatures to return to the warmth of home. 'Feel me,' I say. 'I'm not cold. I want to stay.' My fearlessness frightens him. He sees it as suicidal. He thinks that if I didn't have him with me I would stay out on the isolated hill all night and die. Perhaps he is right. He insists on controlling the situation. He sits beside me, takes my hand, and tells me that we are coming down. And step by step, level by level, he guides me down from my flight until I join him on the ground, cold, shivering, afraid. Now I am more afraid than he is. I don't know where I am. He leads me down from the hill, past houses and people. I am filled with terror. I don't know how he manages to get us back onto the ferry. It is dark now and I grip his hand. As long as I hold onto him the cord of our oneness remains. The minute he lets me go, I panic, so he holds onto me.

We get back to my car and neither of us is capable of driving it. I decide that I should drive it because the car and I understand each other. It is madness. I don't know where I am or where I am going. The streets are just a mass of lights that telescope into each other. I am blind but he knows what to do and he directs me, yard by yard. Somehow we make it back to his place and I collapse onto the floor. We are really coming down now. We relax, talk, listen to music.

Suddenly we are starving and we go out and devour pizzas and talk some more and walk along the streets. Now I no longer need to hold his hand. Now it is time to ask him if he feels a oneness with me, if he believes, as I do, that we have travelled on the same journey. I expect him to deny our union but he does not and I know that, whatever might happen afterwards in our lives, we have shared this very strange day.

We spend one or two nights a week in each other's company but now we have enormous differences. I accuse him of failure to take into account the power of either his own or other people's subconscious minds. I criticize him for following a purely conscious approach in his dependence on astrology. He accuses me of being so involved with self and self-analysis that I never get out into the real world. We disagree, we argue, but we relate to each other.

I make the mistake again of thinking that I love. My children don't like him. He is egotistical, such a centre of the stage person. I am angry with them for not liking him and whenever he is at my house he creates tension between me and my children. He wants to talk to me all the time and has no understanding of the children's needs. I feel used and put upon and torn apart but I let it happen.

There is, about him, a controlled passivity. Every movement he makes and every word that he speaks is slow, deliberate, restrained. I start to feel that a potential violence must dwell beneath his calm façade, a powerful aggression that could erupt at any moment. And there is something about him that is not masculine. It is partly for his feminine qualities that I am attracted to him – for his ability to listen, his love of gossip, his motherly protection of animals and birds who are too weak to help themselves. Though he denies homosexuality, there is something about the way he stands and the way he sits on a chair and in the movement of his hands. Yet the mind is male – incisive, biting, conscious, clever.

I find the relationship disturbing and dissatisfying yet I cling on to it because he constantly challenges and stimulates my mind. I might reject the ideas he presents to me but the important thing is that he gives them. His thinking never stands still so that the conversations range from literature to music to black magic to astrology to the pyramids to the possibility of there being a hole right through the centre of the earth. I never know in advance what the subjects of our discussions will be but I always know that I will be interested.

I have begun to realize, though, that he has a need to have power over people and, although there is still that part of me that wants to be dominated and controlled there is, by now, a well defined area of self that wants to be free. To my great relief he decides to rent a beach house about fifty miles away. I'm glad to see him go and even drive him up there to make sure that he is safely out of the way.

We are to remain friends but I now reject his world and his way. Drugs are not the answer, not for me at any rate. He will go on pursuing truth from above, from a conscious level or from drug-induced planes of perception. I am disappointed to find that his way is not mine. I will have to go back to the labyrinth of my own brain. My inward journey is dark and frightening and I long to hide from many of the things that I come across along the way but inward journeys do, at least for me, have a feeling of truth about them.

Each school holidays the children stay for one week with their father and I make constructive use of these weeks alone – I go away to write, to think, to dream, to sort things out and it seems to me that I am getting somewhere in the struggle towards knowing what I am and what I have been.

I live in the world of the dream. I dream a great deal about my mother as if the answer might lie in the meaning that she and I have for each other. I dream that she and I are seated on the stage of a large auditorium. We are both members of a discussion panel and there is a big audience. She speaks first. She is articulate and forceful but she is wrong and I want to refute what she has to say. I get up to speak but I have no voice at all. I struggle and force the hoarse words out of my mouth but she shouts me down and I am helpless beneath the barrage of her words.

Again I dream that I am taking my children to the pictures and my mother is horrified by the way I am dressed. I am wearing jeans and an old jumper and she says I'll catch cold and die if I go out dressed like that. We argue and I realize how susceptible to death I am if I let go of her values. In the dream I am trying to write and every time that I put out my arm to write a train runs over it. So I give up and stop trying to write. Then my mother puts her whole head under the train, once for each circuit, and her face keeps bouncing back with the mask of a woman – sterile and nondescript, a mockery of woman. She would not have me create. She would like me to be her kind of woman, satisfied with motherhood, a suitable profession and the conventional values of our society. How difficult it is to break free!

Then I dream that I am walking up endless flights of stairs. There are eight flights and I have climbed up seven of them when I come across a madwoman who insists on showing me her son. Her son is a large doll with short, boy's hair but dressed in a white wedding dress with a veil of white netting. And as I watch I see the madwoman killing her baby and I run away because the madwoman is my mother and she is killing me, killing my maleness, killing my aggression, killing my creativity and covering it up with the death mask of the wedding-dress doll. And so I turn and run away. I cannot climb the eighth flight of stairs that perhaps will set me free.

Then I dream that I am going on a journey, carrying all my burdens with me – blankets, pillows, towels. I stop near a caravan to make my bed. I want to lie down and go to sleep but I am surrounded by small, frightening looking animals who keep staring at me and licking me. I feel frightened so I get up and fold up my blankets. Then I fold up all the animals. They looked terrifying but I am able to overcome them easily. They are all the ugly, aggressive feelings that have lived inside of me. Perhaps I am free of my internal, ravenous, aggressive lion.

In my dream the boys and girls who have been sleeping in the caravan suddenly rush out with black, runny faeces pouring down their legs and through their clothes. I go into the caravan and there I see a horrible mess of human and animal faeces. At first I think it's my job to clean up other people's shit but then I take another look and decide that it's not my job at all and I pick up my possessions and walk away. The road ahead of me is long and clear and, although I cannot see over the next hill, I know with certainty that it is the last hill I will have to climb. But my burden is heavy and I curse myself for having carried my blankets and pillows around with me for so long and I know that I'll have to keep carrying them. I will not be free of my mother until I've got over that next hill.

And so I continue to carry my excess weight around with me, a burden of atonement to her for the murderous aggression I felt towards her so long ago – there, at her breast. And I continue to express the vicious forces safely locked within the mountain of my flesh. And I continue to be amorphous, to have no clearly defined boundaries of self, so that I am always vulnerable, wide open to the demands and invasion of others. I seem to choose men who will make those demands, men who will carry out those invasions. Life is difficult, lonely and full of endless tasks and responsibilities.

And as I move in my chair, in the small lounge room of the Paris hotel, I realize that I have changed a great deal. I am here, on the other side of the world, and I'm managing perfectly well. I think I've climbed the last hill, overcome the last impediment. Now perhaps I might love myself.

Now I can't wait to get out of Paris I get up very early and I leave the hotel while it is still dark and I catch a train to Versailles and I forget all about the Frenchman and all the men who have ever asked anything of me. I wander through the Palace, marvelling at its wondrous vulgarity, gaping at its ornate splendour. I walk for hours down through the gardens and by the time I have finished I am numbed by the cold but I feel satisfied with my day. As I catch the train back to Paris the cloud of the Frenchman descends on me and I hope I am going to be able to avoid him.

I return to the hotel and pack my bags so that I am ready to leave although it is much too early yet for me to go. My train does not leave until midnight. He knocks on my door and I let him in. I want to explain to him that making love with him was good but, if we had not made love, that would also have been good. Because of his poor grasp of English it is impossible for me to convey these subtleties to him.

I am determined to retain my individuality and my separateness but, in the end, I am not able to keep hold of my dignity. He doesn't listen to me. He takes off his clothes and gets into bed. He is not at all disturbed by my having disappeared for the day. He no longer talks of finding a way to keep me in Paris. He is, however, quite determined to make love to me once more before I leave and he intends to go with me to the train, to wave me goodbye.

Although he is not being unreasonable I can't do what he wants. I can't do it because I don't want to do it. I refuse him and he is wounded because he cannot understand why I am refusing him. I burst into tears because the assertion of self is such a new thing to me and I don't want to be made to do anything that I don't want to do. While I'm picking up my bags and crying I tell him quickly – so quickly that I know he won't be able to understand my English – that I have been obliged for too many years to do what others wanted and that

I can no longer, no longer, no longer do what a man wants just because he wants it and he doesn't know how to deal with my tears and I leave him lying in bed, naked, the covers drawn up beneath his chin, like a frail and helpless child. An old man unmasked. Last in a line of alien lovers. And I've got what I wanted, haven't I? I've finally won by exercising my will and by seeing him like this – powerless, defenceless, stripped bare, reduced to impotence. I rush from the room and jump into a taxi and flee to the station and I'm shaking, aren't I, with fear and insecurity and razor-edged emotions because I've dared to assert myself and now all I want is to get away, away – from Paris and from the Frenchman and from the past and from myself.

TEN

I arrive at Paris Gare de Lyon still feeling upset and disturbed but relieved at having escaped from the Frenchman. I have plenty of time to spare but when I look at my train ticket I realize that I don't understand it. What do the numbers on my ticket mean? How do I know which train to catch, which carriage to get into, which seat to sit in? I have no idea and I'm not sure what to do. I wander up and down and I find a train with a 'Venezia' sign so I presume this is the one I have to catch, but I decide to go to the information section of the railway station to try to have my ticket explained to me. The man busily tells me that he doesn't speak English and gestures for me to go to a man further down the counter. Struggling with my heavy suitcase, my hand luggage and a bag of food that has to last for the three nights and two days of my train journey, my scarf constantly falling off, my shoulder bag refusing to stay in place and slipping to ground level, I make my way to the man who is supposed to speak English. He tells me, very rudely, that he doesn't speak English and gestures for me to go back the way I came. I feel like crying. Now I wish I had made love to the Frenchman. Then he would have come here with me and his French would have saved me and got me safely onto the train.

I go back to the train. I find a station guard. I show him my ticket and tell him that I don't speak French and that I don't know where to go. He tells me that he doesn't speak English. He spits the words out viciously at me, 'Je ne parle pas Anglais!'

I scream at him, 'You rotten, stinking bastard!' He keeps gesturing me to go further and further up the platform. I crumble into the last carriage, not caring whether it is the right one or not and sit down. A kind, English-speaking, French–speaking

German, who has witnessed both my swearing and my distress explains to me that a part of the train we are travelling on has not yet arrived. He looks at my ticket and shows me that if you lift the top page and look at the carbon underneath then the mysterious numbers fit into boxes clearly showing time, train number, carriage number, seat number. He explains that my carriage is one of those that has not yet arrived.

I wish I were home with my children but I'm not. I'm here in Paris feeling alone and afraid and alienated and I only manage to hold myself together because there's nothing else I can do.

The rest of our train arrives. It is now well past midnight and I just hope that I can keep calm. I must have had some effect on the French station guard because, as soon as the other carriages start to arrive, he comes and takes me to my place.

I feel that I have had enough to put up with but there's more to come. There is a little man in my carriage. He and I are the only ones in it. I realize then, with a kind of shock, that men and women are not separated for sleeping in European trains. I have considered myself to be a liberated woman but the prospect of sharing a sleeping compartment with a total stranger fills me with unknown terrors. But once in bed I feel no fear and I shove earplugs into my ears to shut out the man and the night and the world.

I share my carriage with this little Italian for ten hours. He is going to Milan. In the morning he tries to talk to me but communication is almost impossible. He asks me, in French, if I am married. I tell him that I have children and he wants to see their photographs.

He revolts me. He is ugly and round and about fifty years old. He smokes in our carriage despite the clear non-smoking signs. He eats a bread roll with foul-smelling salami and cheese and then noisily picks his teeth. He snuffles and sniffs and clears his throat a lot. I want to scream. I long to be alone. I take out a book in the hope that I might get lost in it. Though we are the only two people in the carriage he sits right opposite me. I can feel his nearness. Once his leg come close to mine. I hastily move and curl my legs up under me on the seat. I know he is looking at me. I keep reading my book.

I decide to try to blot him out and I lie down on the seat, my coat for a pillow, handbag tightly clutched, and pretend to be asleep. I stay this way for a long time and I can almost imagine that, because I have closed my eyes, he is no longer there. Then I feel something brushing against my shoulder. I open my eyes and see that he is putting on his coat. He says we are approaching Milan and, realizing that I am going to have the carriage to myself, I sit up to say goodbye to him. And then the strangest thing happens. He kneels down in front of me. He looks into my eyes. Delicately, gently, he kisses me on the left cheek and then on the right cheek and then again on the left cheek. He holds my hands and looks at me and says, 'Au revoir. Bon voyage.' And as his grey eyes penetrate mine I see that he is neither ugly nor repulsive but simply a middle-aged man whose naked gaze is saying to me all the things that had not been said and I see that he is mourning the loss of what could have been, but had not been.

The train is late and I start to get anxious. I must change trains at Venice and the night trip through the Swiss Alps has slowed us down. There is ice two feet thick on the roof tops and the train tracks are dangerous and covered with snow. What will happen to me if I miss my train connection at Venice? I have no Italian money and I feel again the overwhelming anxiety that arises out of the inability to speak the language.

Italians get in and out of my carriage as the day proceeds. Some try to speak to me, some ignore me.

When we arrive in Verona, about two hours away from Venice, an Italian gets onto the train and sits next to me. He tells me that he learned English at school about twenty years ago and he seems willing to recall it for my sake. We talk of many things. He is forty-four years old, works as a clerk, studies psychology at night and is married with one sixteen-year-old daughter. He tells me that if he were not married he would have lots of money and would travel all over the world. He asks me if I am married and I tell him I am not but that I have four children. I even try to tell him, in simple words, of my need to be free. I keep thinking that speaking English must be a strain for him so, when the conversation lags, I look out the window and pretend to be watching the scenery. But he keeps asking me questions and he seems to want to talk to me. He tells me that he was born in Trieste and that he goes back there for one month's holiday each year. He takes out a pen and paper and draws a sailing boat to show me what he likes to do. Then he tries to tell me that, because he forty-four, his life is over. He does not hope for a future any longer and tries to express his dissatisfaction and his feeling that it is too late for his life to change. I tell him that I am forty and that I do not feel old and I believe that a new and exciting life is possible for me.

He keeps looking at me and it seems to me that, in spite of his difficulty with English, we are learning something about each other. He tries to teach me some Italian. I tell him that the only Italian I know is 'Arrivederci'. Then he tells me that there is a difference between 'Arrivederci', meaning 'We'll see each other again soon,' and 'Adio', meaning 'Goodbye forever'.

He asks me if he can write something for me. He writes in English, 'You are very …', then pauses and tells me that he will have to finish the sentence in Italian. He adds the word 'sympatica'. 'You are very sympatica,' he says. There is, between us, a moment of strange embarrassment. The train is pulling into Venice and I am overcome again by my anxiety about changing trains. He tells me his name and asks me to write down my name. I do so and then bundle up all my goods. As I struggle down the narrow corridor I hear him call out to me, 'Adio! Adio!' I don't turn back and look at him though I know I should drop my bags and rush back and hug him and say goodbye and kiss him and tell him that he is a man I could have loved. I keep walking. I do not even turn my head.

To my enormous relief the Italian train guard is kind and helpful. The train to Greece has waited the three hours for us. I am immediately taken from one train to the next and shown to my carriage. The train journey seems endless but I don't want to sleep. I want to think about the man who cried when he kissed me goodbye at Sydney airport. I wonder if I will be free of him by the time I get back home. Or will I act out again the destructive games I have played with him over the past few years. My mind goes back to meeting him on the beach two years ago. I am swimming and this man comes up to me.

'Will you teach me how to float?' he asks. I look at him – early thirties, bearded, brown, slim. He's attractive and friendly so I decide to talk to him.

'Why not,' I reply and I try to show him how to float but he's hopeless and we laugh a lot and then go back up onto the beach to talk. As we sit and chat I learn that he comes from

Adelaide and hasn't been in Sydney very long. When he hears that I have children he asks me all about them and seems to be genuinely interested in them. It's Thursday and because I am lonely and he is friendly I invite him to come to dinner on Saturday night. I have to leave then to pick up my kids and I tell him that I'll probably come back to the beach the next day.

I come back to the beach and I see him before he sees me. He's pacing up and down and when he sees me he looks so pleased that I know he's been waiting for me. This eagerness makes him all the more attractive to me and as we sit together on the beach we both know that we will soon be making love. As we leave the beach he says to me, 'I think I should warn you – I've a prick that always stays hard.' It's a long trip home and he follows me in his old tank of a car and all the way I am dreaming of the magic of the prick that always stays hard. It seems so long since I've known real satisfaction.

It is Friday, 11am. My children are with their father and are not due back until Saturday night. We go to bed and we stay there for the whole thirty hours. Within half an hour it is obvious that there is a strong sexual spark between us. But, within a few hours, we realize that it is more than that, much more. There is a perfection of sexual harmony. Though he has been married twice and, to use his words, 'fucked his way around the world three times', he has never met anyone who matches his sexuality as I do. I have, by means of an efficient and co-operative lover, expanded and extended my sexuality to a high degree but I've never know such love making as I know with this man. And it is not just sexual because, after twenty-four hours of passionate encounters, we find ourselves making love in such a way that our physical, sexual, emotional fusion is total.

I hold nothing back, nor does he and we are left shattered by the power of our union so that we both feel that we are in love.

He has nowhere to live so he moves in with me. He has no job so he goes on the dole. He feels guilty about having left his wife in Adelaide and says that he will return there in about six weeks' time, sort out his affairs, and then return to me.

There is no doubt in his mind that he is in love with me. Though he has devoted his life to making love to women, he has never believed in love and is surprised and, indeed, astounded to find that it exists. His joy at discovering what all the love songs are about is both childlike and delightful. He is romantic and gay. He dotes upon me. I cannot wait for the nights to come but must rush home between classes to make love. I long for the days when the children are not there. We are in a constant state of sexual hunger. It only needs a touch, a kiss, a look to fill us with passion. He loves everything about me. He longs for my period to start because it will be something new to savour, to enjoy. My blood is on his tongue and in his mouth and he eats me and drinks me and takes me. And I am lost in the world of his sexuality and mine and I long to stay there forever. Every day, for six weeks, we make love three or four times a day. Our passion feeds upon itself, renews itself, time and time again. Deep within myself I feel that, when he returns to Adelaide, he will stay there and so the days and the weeks are precious to me.

He is all things alien to me. He's an East End Londoner, poorly educated, ex-sailor, ex-badboy, tattoos on his hands. Parents and friends will not approve. I don't care. There is something in me that takes perverse pleasure in caring about the kind of man whom everyone would regard as unsuitable for me. He is childish. He fights with the children over which

TV programme is to be watched. He creates tension between me and the children but he loves me with passion and with devotion. He wants nothing from life but to be my sexual slave forever. And I love the fact that he so loves me.

Then he tells me that he cannot leave me and that he will not return to Adelaide. I'm a bit surprised that I'm disappointed. It is now six weeks since I've known him and I'm ready to move out of the sexual fusion and back into other areas of existence. But he has no other thoughts, no other interests, no other areas of existence to return to and he wants to keep me trapped in the world of our sexuality.

I tell him that I need to feel a sense of space about me and that I cannot possibly live with a man. He will have to move out. He moves out but he spends more nights at my house than he does at his own flat and the battles begin. I try to explain my needs but he refuses to understand and he cannot leave me alone. He is obsessed and I am never alone long enough to get any feeling of my individuality back. It seems like a week to him if he does not see me for one day.

I don't know what to do because I now understand that I have mistaken sexual fusion for love. I'm not in love with him. I don't even respect him but I can't tell him to go away because I know he won't go. It's more than that – part of me doesn't want him to go away. He invites me to dinner at his place and he makes me heart-shaped bread and butter. Where in the world would I find another man who loves me enough to do that?

I wake up each morning dreading that he will be out there, sleeping on the lounge room floor. I am afraid that I will never free myself of him. We fight and argue all the time and then avoid our differences by tumbling into bed, lost in the wonder of our passion and the intensity of our love making. I seem to enjoy provoking his anger and then calming it, momentarily, by means of our sexuality.

He hates my intellect and is jealous of my education. He says I am an intellectual snob but he can't understand my mental capacity and I relish what is, for me, a reversal of roles. In the area of intellect I've at last got a man I can defeat. And I do this purposefully, viciously. I do not like the games I play.

He is not able to understand that love can be stifling, suffocating. All he wants is to love me – what can be wrong in that? It is not possible for him to see that his presence in the house stops me from being myself. He keeps insisting that it should be possible to live together. He invades me, eats his way into my body and into my brain. Again, I find myself defenceless, unable to protect myself from the forced entry of another. I submit to the trembling length of his body against mine, sigh at the moment of our joining, ride and fly and soar until I open like a flower beneath him and take him whole into the centre of my being, until he and I explode as one.

It is three months now since I met him and I am afraid to stop. I am afraid of the violence that might erupt, afraid of what he might do to me if I try to end the relationship. I am bound and held, trapped by the threat of his inner rage. And then he comes to my house, one cold winter night, and swallows a whole bottle of valium tablets. He lies down on the floor and is ready to die. I'm furious with him. How dare he die in my house! I keep him awake and offer to take him to hospital but he refuses to go. He walks out of the house, unloved, unwanted and, as soon as he's left, I call the police and they find him and take him to hospital and his stomach is pumped out.

I don't know what to do. I want him to not exist but he leaves the hospital the next night and comes back to me. All he's ever wanted is just to love me and look what I'm doing to him! I tell him to go away but he refuses. The children are here with me and we are all afraid of him. I try to keep him calm but it's impossible. I've really got myself into a mess this time. He goes into my room and tears up a skirt he bought me. He takes up my son's guitar, which he has been mending and restoring, and smashes it to pieces. He stumbles out of the room, knocking down chairs, scattering papers. He's screaming at me now. 'Look what you've done to me!' he shouts. He's violent now. I'm shaking with terror. I'm sure he'll kill me and my children. And what kind of a mother am I, to have exposed them to this?

I call the police and they come and take him away but the only way in which they will keep him locked up for the night is if I make a charge against him. I do that and I tell the police that he is sick and that he needs psychiatric help. While I am at the Police Station he asks to see me. I don't ever want to see him again but I feel responsible for what's happened to him and the policeman takes me to where he is and I speak to him through the bars of a small opening in the door of his cell. He begs me to bail him out. He says he's been in such places before, been in trouble with the police before, that he can't bear to spend a night in a cell. I tell him I can't do it and as I leave I hear him smash his fist against the door and scream out after me, 'You fuckin' bitch!'

I don't know who to turn to. I cannot tell anyone in my family – I'm too embarrassed and too ashamed of having made such a poor choice. There's to be a court appearance the next morning and the police have assured me that he'll be remanded for psychiatric treatment.

I go to the court the next morning, sure that this is the very last time that I will ever see this man, positive that he will be committed to hospital. But he's not. He's very calm and reasonable. He tells the magistrate that he realizes that he's been a fool. He knows that I do not love him. He won't cause any more trouble and he won't bother me again. He will immediately return to Adelaide where he has a wife, a home, a job. My God! They believe him! Worse, I believe him. I leave the court and get into my car. He asks if he can speak to me for a moment. I refuse. Just for a moment. Then I agree. He gets into the car. He starts to cry. 'I just love you so much,' he weeps. 'I can't leave you.' I am the one in the prison cell.

I jump out of the car and rush back into the court and, although there's another case being heard, I interrupt and cry out, 'Won't somebody help me?' I tell them that he's lied. That he's not going back to Adelaide, that I'm afraid of him. There is nothing they can do to help me. The magistrate has made his decision and that, apparently, is that. Two policemen come outside with me but, by now, both he and my car have disappeared. I'm frightened that he's gone to my house and the children are there alone. A policeman drives me home and there he is, gently and softly holding my sons, telling them how sorry he is to have frightened them, crying, begging their forgiveness.

'Will you come with me to the hospital,' I beg him. 'You need help.' He is very quiet now and he agrees. We go to the psychiatric hospital and I'm horrified by their indifference.

'There's nothing wrong with him,' the doctor tells me. 'He's just in love with you.' But I know it's more than that. He's not just in love with me. He's abnormally obsessed with me. I realize that I might be stuck with him for life but I know that I've got myself into this destructive situation and I've got to try to get myself out of it. My children are on school holidays and are to go to stay with their father for a week. I decide to make a last effort to help this man. I tell him I'll give him one week to pull himself together. Then he has to move back to his own place and get a job and look after himself.

I nurse him for a week, marvelling again at the way I seem to involve myself in relationships that seem designed to annihilate me. The week is one of total giving on my part but he responds and gets himself together and does what I ask.

We go on then, in some kind of way. Our relationship is full of arguments in which we behave like infants, picking at and disparaging each other and then forgetting about our differences in the only way we know how – by a submission to the oneness of our sexual union.

I refuse, in a sense, to compromise. I will not marry him and I will not live with him and I go on insisting upon my need to live alone with the children, to be myself, to write. However, I spend so much time arguing with him about my need to write that there is no time left to do it. I am constantly afraid of what he might do if I end the relationship completely. So we go on destroying each other, month after month after month.

As I think of him now I see our relationship with great clarity. It has been a continuation of my constant involvement with dominating and potentially destructive men. I have been attracted to, and held by, his violence. I have wanted to test his aggression, to play with it, to see what limits it has. If his destructive forces have limits, can be contained, then perhaps the same will be true of mine. I pretend to myself that it is sexuality, the power of the penis that I want to have and to control – but it is not. I want a greater power than that. I want to be omnipotent. I want to control the murderous rage of others. If I can do that, then perhaps I will be able to control my own. And now, armed with this knowledge and my new-found love and respect for myself, I realize it is possible to break the relentless pattern, to set myself free and to keep myself free of dangerous and destructive relationships. I am ready for the last stage of my journey.

ELEVEN

As soon as I arrive in Athens I feel that I have come to a place where I belong. Greece is the country I have wanted most to see. There is no fantasy of a charming Greek Knight in Shining Armour. I have come to accept that Knights in Shining Armour do not exist. There is, instead, an intuitive feeling that Greece will provide an important experience for me.

The first day is exciting: I go exploring and find myself in the Plaka and wander in and out of all the market shops. The next day the weather is perfect: sunny and not too cold and I climb the Acropolis. It is the fulfilling of a life ambition – to stand at the top of the Acropolis, to see, in reality, the wonder of ancient Greece, to touch the stones, to dream, to be a part of myth.

And as I stand here, on top of this mighty mountain, I feel the power of Athena as if her vigour were my own. Here she stood, dwelt in this citadel – born fully armed from the head of Zeus yet warlike only in defending her household, inventor of the olive, wise in counsel, goddess of arts and goddess of work, mountain-mother of the people. And she did not humble herself before god or man. She did not submit to the rape of Hephaistos but collected his seed from the ground thus achieving motherhood while retaining her virginity. I wonder if it's too late to become a serene, all-giving, virgin-mother. The calm majesty of Athena rests upon the mountain and on me.

The next day I go off on a bus trip to Cape Sounian and I am again moved to find that myth can come alive for me. I can see Aegeus waiting for the return of his son, feel his despair as he sees the black sails of the approaching ship, identify with the agony of believing that his son is dead, throw myself with him off the cliffs of Sounian. It is not myth. It must have happened.

The guide shows me the place, on a marble column, where the poet Byron scratched his name.

The next day I go down to the harbour at Piraeus and take a boat ride to one of the closer islands. On the trip back my attention is attracted by a Greek family – a mother, a father and two little boys. She is young, very dark-skinned, classically beautiful. He has slightly grey hair, lighter colouring, a finely chiselled face. I cannot stop looking at them because they all love each other so much. It is a long trip and the little boys fall asleep. Then she lays her head lovingly on her husband's shoulder and they kiss and touch and caress. I feel jealous. Is it possible, after all, for marriage to work? But there is no shoulder for me to lay my head on, no warm husband for me to caress.

We get close to the harbour and she gets up and wakes her children. They grizzle a bit and she cuddles them and kisses them into good humour. The husband watches her. As the boat pulls into the wharf she gets up, ready to disembark. She has a child on either side of her, holding a hand of each. Then he gets up behind her and my mind is momentarily unable to take in what my eyes are seeing. When he stands I see that he is a midget. His face is of normal adult size but his body, though well proportioned, is tiny, infant-sized. Here, indeed, is love. Tears come into my eyes.

Then I set off with enthusiasm for a four-day trip to the ancient Greek sites. It is winter time and there are very few tourists, only fifteen on our bus. Although most of my fellow-travellers are Australian teachers only one of them understands what Greece means to me. He and I become friends and we are constantly high on the marvels of ancient Greece. His interest is in history, mine in myth.

Our guide is wise and talented and well able to make the past live again. We visit Corinth and Olympia. I long to climb the mountain behind the ancient city of Corinth but there's not enough time. I'll do it one day. I already know that I'll come back to Greece. What I see doesn't matter as much as how I feel. I learn that the secret of myth is that you cannot distinguish it from reality. Myth is real. It is not just a story that Athena inhabited these woods – she did live here. Oedipus really did meet and kill his father at this very spot, where the three roads meet. The fortresses, the giant theatre at Epidaurus, the ancient tombs of Mycenae – they live for me and I am part of them. History, myth, reality – moulded into one.

And then we approach Delphi and I know that this is the place I have struggled to find. The sea of olive trees spreads before me as we wind our way round the steep mountains and we arrive at Delphi, the giant symbolic navel of the world. What incentive they must have had, those ancient Greeks, to journey across such inhospitable mountains to congregate in Delphi. And yet, I understand why they did so for Delphi is a magical place. As I climb the mountain and the winter mists descend about me I can feel my union with the spirit of myth that was and that is and that will be. I am no longer a child, bound to its mother by the uncut cord. I am, instead, invisibly bound to Delphi, to the navel of Mother Earth. Delphi is, above all, a female place. The Oracle is a woman and she knows the mysteries. Her secrets pulsate with vigorous force in the womb of every woman. I sit alone on the mountain – elated, exhilarated, rejoicing in the knowledge of my inner female strength. I have, within me, the power to murder or the power to create and as I get up and make my slow way down the mountain side, I know that I have, finally, made my choice.

I am not sorry to leave Greece. I want to go home. I need my children, their love and their warmth. Everything moves in speeded-up time. An uneventful train trip to Venice, a day to explore this fairy-tale city, a two-day trip to Paris, a hovercraft crossing to London, one day in London, onto the plane and on my way home.

I sit on the plane and try to take stock of what has happened to me. I've gone to the other side of the world alone and survived. I have learned that it's possible to eat like a normal human being. I have learned that being alone does not mean that one needs to be lonely. I have learned that I can do without men. And I've started to love myself.

In a state of smug self-satisfaction I let myself drift into sleep. And then I dream the dream of the ferry boat. In my dream my children and I and all my family, my husband, my lovers and all the men I've known, are going on a ferry ride. We are going to Bondi Beach for a picnic. Although I alone am responsible for my children, the responsibility causes me no anxiety. They are off playing somewhere on the ferry. I can look out to see and feel the breeze and the exhilaration of the journey. We arrive at the beach and the children go into the ocean to swim. I notice one little blonde girl go in and immediately drown in the waves but I feel no concern for my own children. I know they are safe, way out there somewhere in the ocean, swimming happily. They are no burden to me and I can relax and swim and lie in the sun. Then the picnic is over and we must get back onto the ferry and go home. Again the children leave me alone and I go to pay the ferryman for our ride. I take out my purse and it is full of coins. I pay him for myself and for my children but he laughs at me. He tells me that I've paid too much and he returns some money to me so that my purse is overflowing with exotic, foreign coins. As we get off the ferry I realize, again, how little trouble the children have been.

Then the scene changes and I am in a hospital room. But I am not there because I am sick. I have gone there to write a book. The room I am in has no walls and no ceiling. It is completely open and people come and go busily and, yet, I feel content amid all this activity, quite sure that I will be able to get on with my writing.

Then I begin to feel some anxiety. I know that, during the day, I will be alright but I do not know about the night. All this activity will cease and the people in the beds around me will be asleep and I will be disturbed by their snoring, intruded upon by their breathing. Suddenly I wish I had some earplugs.

A lady walks by with a trolley of chemist shop goods for sale. She puts beautifully packaged soap and talcum powder on my bed but I am not interested in these and I ask her if she has some pure, herbal soap to wash myself with. She does and I buy it. I wonder if she will think I'm crazy if I ask her for earplugs. I decide to ask and she surprises me by having some and I buy them from her. Then I feel perfectly happy.

The dream is a very satisfying one for me. I see in it that my children can be my fellow-travellers in life and not my burdens. I see also that, no matter what activities and intrusions surround me, it will always be possible to construct for myself my own walls, my own space, my own area of self in which I can be alone and write.

The plane touches down and I can think only of my children. My lips need to kiss them, my arms want to hold them. I leave Customs, laden down with bags. Despite the crowds of people I know exactly where to look as I identify their voices calling, 'Mummy! Mummy!' I do not intend to cry but I do as we hug and kiss and chatter. Their faces look strange to me. I suppose that mine looks strange to them. They start telling me all that has happened in the last six weeks. I hear, but do not listen to, their words. I look up and I see my parents. She, who could not come to see me off, has come to welcome me home. I find that it is, after all, not difficult to hug and kiss her. She looks at me and, to my great surprise, I see that she loves me. I smile at her and she smiles at me and I feel that my struggle is over. And as I look at her I realize that the answer does not lie in the seeing or the knowing or the understanding of self. These are necessary tools but they cannot set you free. Growing up is largely a matter of being able to forgive.

I walk back to the car with the four children that I love and, as we walk happily along, the dream of the ferry ride comes back into my mind. I've been on my journey. I've travelled through the mists to the dark mouth of Hades but I'm not dead. Life hasn't ended. It's still going on. And I've paid too many coins to the ferryman. The rest of my journey is free.

Also available from Leone Sperling

MOTHER'S DAY

HATE

This is the story of a mother and daughter who hated each other with great passion. They would, if they could, have carved each other up into pieces and thrown the pieces into garbage bags and hurled the garbage bags into the sea. And they would, if possible, have sawed up each other's bones to make sure that there was no chance of resurrection.

They were not aware of their hatred for each other. They would have been surprised to learn that, beneath the flooding warmth of love, there grew an ugly thing of such diabolic power that it needed only the touch of one man to bring it to monstrous life.

A man entered their lives and fed their fire and touched off their tragedy until it had no choice but to hurl itself to its determined end.

EVE

Tragedy makes no sense if you look at it in isolation. Murder is meaningless unless you see it as the ultimate act of self immolation and so it is necessary to look at Eve – slim-hipped, narrow-pelvised. Skinny, you would call her if you saw her gliding down the street. Long, frizzy, mousy hair she has and her top teeth protrude. Her narrow lips cannot cover this projection and, in repose, her upper teeth rest on her lower lip. And the protrusion of the teeth is uneven so that the curve is more obvious on the right hand side of her face. It is not unattractive and rest of her face is lean and smooth and white. She has light brown eyes and a long, thin neck. Her hands are slender and delicate. Her breasts are small and her hips don't curve and yet she carries herself, as she walks down the street, with a feminine elegance and grace. Eve.

EVE AND THE BABY

The most significant thing about Eve, a thing you would not notice immediately, is that she is carrying a baby. The baby is glued into her neck so tightly that you would be forgiven if you did not notice it at all. Once someone stopped her in the street and asked to see the baby. She had to pull the baby off her and turn it to the sun for inspection. It was a very difficult thing to do. It was difficult for Eve and it was difficult for the baby because they were inseparable and whenever there was a space between them their bodies felt as if they had been peeled raw and they were both drawn by a magnetic need to get their skins back together again. The person who asked to see the baby did not understand this. In fact the person was so insensitive as to ask Eve what the baby's name was. Quite understandably, Eve was shocked. The baby had no name. How can you give a separate name to a small area of you own skin?

THE BABY

And how did the baby feel about all of this? The baby felt just fine. It was a very lucky baby. For most of us birth means the beginning of being alone. This baby was never alone. Eve had given her baby an outside womb and the baby, naturally enough, was content to stay there. And who can blame the baby for that? Being happy, resting snug forever in its warm mother womb.

ORDER

Eve was a hermit. No doubt, once upon a time, she had a mother and a father. Perhaps she had a sister or a brother. Long ago, there must have been laughter and tears. Certainly she had known passion and despair, heartbreak and happiness, pain and joy but she had decided, for some reason, that the world of men and women was not for her. The only problem attached to such a decision was that, deep within her, she felt an aching urgency to bear a child and so she went out into the world and got pregnant as quickly as possible and, as soon as she was certain that the child was growing there, inside her womb, she locked herself away again.

She lived in a small house, with a small garden and everything in her house and in her garden was perfectly in order. Neat and flawless, tidy and clean. She could not tolerate chaos. Perhaps that is why she found the world of men and women so distasteful.

She saw that there was some kind of pattern in the universe and she attempted to take this order and distill it and extract its essence and pour it into her house and into her garden and into her womb.

Eve never allowed the slightest thing to disturb her. She maintained, at all times, a sense of harmonious equilibrium, a cool and balanced calm.

She had no telephone and if anyone dared to knock on her door she simply behaved as if they hadn't knocked at all. She had the power to annihilate anyone.

People thought she was peculiar.

ROTTEN LITTLE BASTARD

At the same time, a few hundred miles away, in the children's ward of a hospital devoted to treating sufferers of tuberculosis, a five-year-old boy was visiting his eight-year-old girlfriend. He was supposed to stay in his own bed but some inner compulsion kept drawing him to hers. He would lie in the crook of her mothering arm, his little cheek resting on her chest, his arm across her belly. Every now and then she would nuzzle into him and kiss him on the lips His stiff little prick lay exquisitely on her thigh. Sometimes she would put her hand down underneath the covers and let her pudgy fingers touch his erection. When she did this he was suffused with an indescribable feeling for which he did not have a name. Sometimes she took his left hand and placed it on her gently swelling mound and they rested like that for a long time. They could have stayed that way forever.

The nursing staff did not approve of this kind of behaviour and whenever they came across our cuddling couple, cocooned in ecstasy, the nurses would shout at them and tear them viciously apart and smack his bum and send him crying back to bed and say, 'You rotten little bastard!' No one blamed the girl.

Sometimes he would hide in the girls' toilets and wait for the girl to come in. When he heard the tinkle of her pee in the toilet, his penis would grow stiff and he would rub it – up and down, up and down, up and down. He didn't know why. He would have liked her to pee all over him.

MOTHER'S DAY
is available for Kindle, iBooks and POD at

www.cilentopublishing.com

AUTHOR'S BIOGRAPHY

Leone Sperling was born in Sydney in 1937, attended Sydney Girls' High School and graduated from Sydney University with a BA Honours degree in English literature. She taught English full-time with the NSW Department of TAFE for twenty years, a career that she found rewarding and fulfilling. She regards the fact that she did find time to write as a minor miracle because her marriage ended when her children were very young.

Three books, *Coins for the Ferryman*, *Mother's Day* and *Oasis* were published between 1981 and 1990. She was awarded a Literature Board grant in 1985. She has also had several short stories and articles published in national newspapers and Australian anthologies. These are now collected in *The Book of Life*.

After taking early retirement she wrote two novels, *What About Love?* and *Jamie*. She then undertook a four-year naturopathic Diploma in Nutrition. Leone now enjoys close, mutually rewarding relationships with her four children and six grandchildren and studies Latin with Continuing Education at Sydney University. Severe hearing impairment has resulted in the need for a Cochlear implant. For several years Leone has been on the Management Committee of Better Hearing Australia's Sydney branch and spends a considerable amount of time as a research volunteer with Cochlear and with the National Acoustic Laboratories.

Leone's writing is open and honest. Her style is spare and simple but constantly displays a willingness to confront and examine both the joyful and the darker aspects of human emotions and relationships.

www.ingramcontent.com/pod-product-compliance
Lightning Source LLC
Chambersburg PA
CBHW060434180626
46817CB00007B/2805